Poems, Stories

MARGARET TAIT was a filmmaker a.
books of poetry and two collections of short stories (one of them
for children), and made thirty-two short films and the feature-
length *Blue Black Permanent* (1992). She was born in Orkney in 1918.
After qualifying in medicine at Edinburgh University in 1941, she
joined the Royal Army Medical Corps, serving in India, Sri Lanka
and Malaya, before returning to Orkney in 1946. She then studied
in Italy, learning Italian at Perugia's School for Foreigners and,
from 1950 to 1952 studying filmmaking at the Centro Sperimentale
di Cinematografia in Rome. On her return to Scotland, Tait estab-
lished her own film company, Ancona Films, in Edinburgh. In the
1960s she moved back to her native Orkney where she continued
to make films until her death in 1999.

SARAH NEELY is a member of the Stirling Media Research Institute
and a lecturer in Film in the School of Arts and Humanities at the
University of Stirling. Her research stretches across a range of
areas of film and media studies and her most recent work focuses
on Scottish cinema and experimental film. She has researched and
written on the work of Margaret Tait for several years.

ALI SMITH's most recent novel is *There But For The* (Hamish
Hamilton, 2011).

FyfieldBooks aim to make available some of the great classics of British and European literature in clear, affordable formats, and to restore often neglected writers to their place in literary tradition.

FyfieldBooks take their name from the Fyfield elm in Matthew Arnold's 'Scholar Gypsy' and 'Thyrsis'. The tree stood not far from the village where the series was originally devised in 1971.

> *Roam on! The light we sought is shining still.*
> *Dost thou ask proof? Our tree yet crowns the hill,*
> *Our Scholar travels yet the loved hill-side*

from 'Thyrsis'

MARGARET TAIT

Poems, Stories and Writings

Edited with an introduction by
SARAH NEELY
with a Foreword by
ALI SMITH

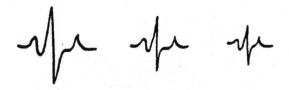

Fyfield*Books*

CARCANET

First published in Great Britain in 2012 by
Carcanet Press Limited
Alliance House
Cross Street
Manchester M2 7AQ

www.carcanet.co.uk

A CIP catalogue record for this book is available from the British Library

ISBN 978 1 84777 159 9

The publisher acknowledges financial assistance from Arts Council England

Supported by
ARTS COUNCIL
ENGLAND

Typeset by XL Publishing Services, Tiverton
Printed and bound in England by SRP Ltd, Exeter

Royalties from this book will be donated to the Orkney archive for the preservation and cataloguing of the Margaret Tait collection.

Contents

POEMS

from origins and elements (1959)

Uncollected and Unpublished Poems

Illustrations

The title page reproduces the heartbeat emblem which Margaret Tait used in her three poetry collections.

Acknowledgements

This collection came to fruition with the support and advice of many. Alan Riach deserves special thanks for suggesting that I approach Carcanet with Tait's poetry in the first place. Carcanet's suggestions for the volume and in particular, Judith Willson's attentive eye, have been a great reassurance. The introduction builds on a number of years of research and owes much to discussions and advice from colleagues in film studies, including Maeve Connolly, Phil Drake, Ian Goode, Lucy Reynolds, Jane Sillars, Sarah Smith and Maggie Sweeney. I am also indebted to the input offered by those who knew Tait personally, or who are particularly close to Tait's work, such as Ute Aurand, Benjamin Cook, Neil Firth, Ola Gorie, Andrew Parkinson, Michael Romer and Gerda Stevenson and Peter Todd, who has offered support throughout the project, including invaluable advice during the final editing phase of the manuscript. The AHRC Early Career Research Fellowship scheme enabled me to give the project the concentrated attention it deserved. And I am also grateful for the encouragement and support of friends, family, in particular, my husband, Robert Anderson.

The volume itself is enriched by many images, some from Tait's films (for which I'm indebted to Scottish Screen Archive), and others – namely photographs of Tait – generously provided by Richard Demarco's Digital Archives and Gunnie Moberg's collection at the Orkney Archive, on behalf of Tam MacPhail.

The work of Alison Fraser, Lucy Gibbon, David Mackie and Sarah MacLean, staff at the Orkney Archive where Tait's collection is housed, has also been instrumental to the completion of this book.

Finally, I would like to extend my gratitude to Margaret Tait's family in Orkney: Peter and Ann Tait, for their hospitality and kindness, and Tait's husband, Alex Pirie, for his continual encouragement and astute advice, and for providing access to a great range of material relating to Tait. Tait's archive, reflecting her life and work as a writer and filmmaker, is inspirational. I hope this collection succeeds in at least providing a glimpse into its full richness.

Sarah Neely

Margaret Tait at Slow Bend, Helmsdale, 1960s.
Copyright © Alex Pirie

Foreword

Here at last is a fuller picture of Margaret Tait, Scotland's original film-poet. We've lacked, until now, a more fully contextualised take on the presence, time and work, in Rome, Perugia, Edinburgh and finally at home in Orkney, of this most bafflingly overlooked of Scotland's versatile twentieth-century artists, and one of the truly neglected aspects of her work is now addressed by this focus on her writing over the decades.

The poems are a revelation in so many ways, of her voice, her eye, her way with edit, her playful idiosyncrasy, her craft, her timing. They reveal her sources: the Bible, myth, medieval ballad, folk form and popular song, united with a modern legacy of breath-rhythm, directness of voice and openness of form characteristic of writers as vibrant and shapeshifting as Whitman, Hopkins, Lorca and Ginsberg, as argumentative, spontaneous-seeming and energetic as D.H. Lawrence (whose empathy, for instance, she emulates and simultaneously, very enjoyably, takes to task). They reveal her, again, as a foreteller of Scottish writers who came decades after her. A Buddhist combination of the meditative with the momentary and an understanding of the layering of time which makes any immediacy, of the 'heritage' in 'brief being', foretells the thoughtful joy in Alan Spence's work. The sense of discursive movement in the poems which makes them dialogues in themselves, their understanding of the vast planet and of the detail of the tiny ceremonies of nature, their playful acuity with local idiom is shared with the late, great Edwin Morgan. The unadorned and thoughtful address, at once disciplined and layered in its distillation, and unfussy and attentive in register, pre-dates something shared, recognisable, even familial, in the voices, found and forged years afterwards, of crucial figures of the late twentieth-century Scottish poetic landscape like Liz Lochhead and Jackie Kay.

'Hold it – Hold it simple – Hold it direct', as she says, late in life, about her film-work. The same applies to her written work, her handling of what she calls the 'delicacy' of words, a delicacy she meets with both subtlety and robustness. Through all her work runs a keen understanding of private space in a public world – this, in part, is what cinema is, for Tait: a way to hold and to connect, in the same moment, the separate individual and the shared, wide-open experience. The short stories included here are another revelation, of her calm observational combination of irony and acceptance and her inquiry into this outsider / insider status. The collected short prose pieces, descriptive of her time in Italy at the Centro Sperimentale in Rome, of her pioneering Rose Street Film Festivals, of her thoughts, in earlier and in later life, about what it means to make anything at all, are not just aesthetically but historically invaluable.

But then, Tait is very concerned with the concept of time, with what it is, and with the usefulness of her own work, not just when it came to banishing or challenging historic and contemporary preconceptions, but also to the constant making-new she perceived as the heartbeat of the poetic act, verbal and visual. 'Each new moment is a new moment.' She is fiercely intelligent, innovative, instinctual; a thinking, feeling poet whose generosity lies in her combining of action and humility, presence and absence: 'Starlings wheel / And know which moment to.'

Informed by a profound, commonsensical proto-feminism; wry to the point of hilarity; mischievous and anarchic; often recalci-trant as if in constant dialogue with herself about the ever-more-openness which ought to characterise her own response – take the way the poem called 'Responsiveness' celebrates how a foot simply hits the ground every time you take a step forward – Tait the writer is a force of shrewd joy in riposte, a force of energy in inquiry. She knows the power of the North; she knows the powers of her Scotland for good and for ill. Her work, so consciously and kickingly anti-Presbyterian, keen to un-repress and un-fix, so concerned, at the same time, with the relationship between truth and sight, makes for a fluidity between nature, reality and art, a world delivered alive, as it is and as it can be imagined, re-seen and re-evaluated with freshness.

'In poetry, something else happens… Presence, let's say, soul or spirit, an empathy with whatever it is that's dwelt upon, feeling for it, to the point of identification.' It's good at last to have this book dedicated to Margaret Tait's writing: this wise reminder, the open invitation to be present, to concentrate, to connect, to let what's there enter as it is, full of its own possibility and ours, at the eye.

Ali Smith, December 2011

Introduction

Margaret Tait is best known for her work as a filmmaker. She worked for the most part independently, producing short, experimental films. When Tait was invited to screen her films at Calton Studios in Edinburgh in 1979, she was billed as a 'one woman film-industry'.[1] Hugh MacDiarmid, of whom Tait produced a film portrait in 1964, described Tait as 'ploughing a lonely furrow'.[2] She scripted, shot and edited her own work, with occasional input from composers for the soundtrack. Films were also sent away to labs for processing, but even then, Tait involved herself heavily in this process, making copious notes regarding what the film should look like and sending films back if they didn't meet with her expectations. These detailed notes would eventually assist the Scottish Screen Archive in their restoration of Tait's films between 1999 and 2004. The films' restoration, the subsequent retrospective and touring programme curated by Peter Todd, for the Edinburgh Film Festival and LUX respectively in 2004, went a long way in raising the profile of the substantial body of groundbreaking work from a filmmaker about whom, until that point, little had been written.

While the influence of poets and poetry on Tait's films is now widely recognised, her own short stories, prose, scripts and poetry are not well known. This collection sets out to introduce readers to the full range of Tait's engagement with poetic forms on the page. It is hoped that this additional context will give a clearer understanding of Tait's filmmaking methods and the importance of her writing within this process. The inclusion of stills from her films is intended to suggest some of these connections. This is by no means a collected works, though. Tait was a prolific writer and her archive contains a wealth of published and unpublished essays, plays, film scripts, novels, short stories and poems. She experimented in a wide range of forms, publishing three collections of poetry, a book of short stories and even a collection of stories for children.[3]

1

Margaret Tait was born in Orkney in 1918. From the age of eight, she was sent to school in Edinburgh where she would remain, studying medicine at Edinburgh University, until she joined the Royal Army Medical Corps in 1943. Throughout her service in India, Sri Lanka and Malaya, Tait demonstrated an interest in photography, taking numerous photographs. It was also during this time that she began focusing on writing up some of her experiences in script and novel form. Her poem, 'Then, Oh Then, Oh Then', included in this collection (p. 62) is dedicated to T.D. ApI, Trevor Dennis ApIvor, a fellow physician whom Tait met in the RAMC. ApIvor later developed a distinguished career as a Welsh modernist composer.

In 1946, Tait returned to the UK and continued work as a physician, living first in Edinburgh, then moving to various locations in England and Wales. From 1946 to 1947, she enrolled in an evening class at Edinburgh College of Art. The following year, when she was living in London, she became involved in a scriptwriting club. In 1950, she studied Italian in Perugia at the University for Foreigners and, from 1950 to 1952, she studied filmmaking at the Centro Sperimentale di Cinematografia in Rome. It was a period greatly influenced by Neorealist approaches to cinema. The movement's commitment to representing the realities of working-class life was admired by Tait, but its approach was never wholly adopted in her own work. Tait explains:

> I was in any case a bit sceptical about neo-realism as almost a sort of creed – as it was to some people. I did like the use of actual locations, but I've always had, too, an enormous admiration for utterly stylised films, studio-made and professionally performed. If you think of Vigo, for instance, I prefer *L'Atalante* and *Zero de Conduite* to *A Propos de Nice* – *L'Atalante* is one of my favourite films – the scene of the wedding party walking down a slope from the church to the barge especially.[4]

Even so, visits from prominent filmmakers of the day at the film school left a lasting impression on Tait. An account of her questioning of Roberto Rossellini during his visit is reprinted in this volume (p. 150).

At the film school in Rome, Tait collaborated with fellow students Fernando Birri and Peter Hollander in the silent film *One is One* (1951). Her reflections on this experience are documented in an article written at the request of Gavin Lambert (then editor of *Sight and Sound*) in 1952, also included in this collection (p. 152).[5] Birri was an Argentinian poet and playwright, while Hollander was an American citizen on a Fulbright scholarship. Birri stayed on in Italy, establishing himself as a filmmaker. He later became a key figure in the establishment of the International School of Film and Television in Cuba, along with Gabriel García Márquez and Julio García Espinosa. After finishing his studies at Centro, Hollander returned to the United States where he worked for WGBH public television in Boston and later made films for the United Nations in New York.

Tait described *One is One* as an 'international collaboration'. Because equipment was in such high demand at Centro, overseas students were not given ready access to it for their own film-making endeavors. This prompted Tait to purchase a Paillard-Bolex from a side-street in Rome, a camera she would use throughout most of her career, replacing it only once in the 1990s as she made her last film, *Garden Pieces* (1998). But for Tait, *One is One* was seen 'chiefly as an exercise'. Another film she made at this time, *Three Portrait Sketches* (1951), she similarly referred to as a 'study in technique'. It starred Birri and Saulat Rahman, a fellow student who would go on to undertake pioneering work in film education in India.

Tait's next film, co-directed with Hollander, *The Lion, the Griffin, and the Kangaroo* (1952) was viewed as a more professional endeavour, with funding secured from the University for Foreigners in Perugia, the United States Information Service and the American Commission for Cultural Exchange. The film largely promotes the university, depicting life as a student. The musical soundtrack features an octet by Ulysses Kay, an African-American Fulbright student at the American Academy in Rome, who went on to lead a distinguished career as a composer, conductor and professor of music.

The impact of the time Tait spent at the film school in Rome resonated throughout her life. In Italy, she founded Ancona Films with Peter Hollander and Fernando Birri. Although eventually Ancona was largely led by Tait with some input by Hollander, initial promotional material for Ancona Films, such as stationery and business cards, listed offices in New York, Rome and Edinburgh. The intention was to establish an international network for the distribution of films by fellow filmmakers. Ancona's Edinburgh headquarters were at 91 Rose Street, where

Tait remained a tenant until 1973. Rose Street, at that time, was a hub of much literary and artistic activity. After Rome, Tait's focus shifted almost entirely to artistic endeavours. Although she continued to work as a locum doctor in the late 1950s and 60s, this was seen as a necessity to enable her to continue as a filmmaker.

The time following Tait's return from Rome, from the mid 1950s to the early 1960s also represented one of the most prolific periods for her writing. This may be partly explained by the fact that on her return to Edinburgh, she was unable to establish a network of support for her filmmaking activities comparable to the one she had so richly drawn from in Rome. Although she was able to eventually develop her own independent way of making films, writing seemed to serve as a more dependable outlet for her creativity at this time. For the most part, she wrote poetry. She also wrote extensively in notebooks and diaries. All activities, like her filmmaking activities, focused on articulating a degree of emotional truth. This could be seen as the point at which Tait was forced to depart from any affiliation with the Neorealist film movement. For Tait, it wasn't reality as seen that held the truth, but reality as felt.

It was a time of great change and unrest for her, lived largely in transit, travelling between locum positions situated throughout the UK, the Rose Street studio, the family home in Orkney and, eventually in the early 1960s, a residence in Sutherland. She travelled a lot by car (specifically, her Ancona Films van), occasionally sleeping in it overnight. Tait embraced the nomadic lifestyle and kept a vivid account of the period in her notebooks, writing often of her preference for living in her car rather than being tied down to a permanent residence. In a letter to her partner Alex Pirie[6] in November 1960, recounting a visit to Hugh MacDiarmid and his wife Valda at Brownsbank, just outside of Biggar, Tait describes how she:

> slept in the car in the field under the pine trees. It was nice to be with them for evening and breakfast. I picked some raspberries at the roadside and got soaked to the skin before returning to Edinburgh.
>
> I was sleeping out in the dark – or in the moonlight – for some days, nights I mean, and will again. It's not sentimentalism, nor even superstition but the spirits under the tree are good for me, I think.[7]

Her unsettled existence fuelled her writing; she records writing two or more poems a day.

Tait left Edinburgh and Rose Street in the mid-late 1960s, living first in Helmsdale in Sutherland, before returning to Orkney in the late 1960s, where she would remain for the rest of her life. Orkney, like Edinburgh, has its own rich literary heritage, although Tait's connection with it is less obvious. She was acquainted with George Mackay Brown, both as a person and through his writing; however, she had no great affinity with his work. Her curt piece in *Chapman*, written in 1996 in remembrance of Mackay Brown, describes him somewhat detachedly as 'always very affable'.[8] She was also acquainted with Edwin and Willa Muir. An admirer of Muir's poetry, in her notebooks Tait refers to a 'gentleness' and a 'strong irony which MacDiarmid doesn't seem to appreciate'.[9]

And Tait's poem, 'Concha Orcadensis', expresses her respect for the Orcadian poet, essayist and naturalist Robert Rendall. In a letter to Alex Pirie, Tait asks:

> I wonder if you will like this brief portrait of Robert Rendall, which I wrote last night. He's a draper in Kirkwall, smallish, round-headed, black-coated, about 77 yrs of age (Kulgin[10] always speaks of him as a 'boy' which makes me laugh) and stone deaf. He writes some verse which sounds good and strong when he speaks it himself. He is a Plymouth Brother, very strict, writes books about God (Jehovah) too, and he studies molluscs. He loves to prowl about the ebb. One of his books of poems is called 'The Orkney Shore.'[11]

Tait's poem on Rendall would later in appear in a programme for BBC radio, produced by George Bruce and Stewart and transmitted on 27 May, 1962. The programme, given the same title as Rendall's collection *The Orkney Shore*,[12] largely focuses on the work and biographies of Rendall, Muir and Mackay Brown. The reading of Tait's own work seems to be included as supplementary, more as an illustration of Rendall, than for any real consideration of her merits as a poet. Tait has regularly been cast in this way: a diminutive figure among the more dominant characters in the landscape of Orcadian poetry. Even in recent years, the most comprehensive history of Orcadian literature overlooks Tait altogether, making no mention of her work.[13]

Tait had more of an affinity with lesser-known women poets such as her sister-in-law, Allison Leonard Tait, and Ann Scott-Moncrieff. Allison Leonard Tait provided Tait with an editor and a sounding board for her work.[14] Leonard Tait's poetry, like Scott-Moncrieff's, was published by Ernest Marwick in his *Anthology of*

Orkney Verse (1949).[15] As Leonard Tait's poem 'Gold'[16] illustrates, the two Taits shared a poetic concern with capturing the ineffable qualities of the present moment:

Gold

Above my head the poppies blow
Their powdered glory to and fro.
Down on my eyelids flecked with gold
Dust of sleep
The sunlight pours.
The golden hours
Slip past me
On fair, unsandalled, soundless feet.
I do not ask the way they go:
Today I watch the poppies blow.

Allison Tait, close in age to Margaret Tait, was the editor of *The Kirkwallian,* the magazine in which some of her poems were published. She also studied literature at the University of Edinburgh in the late 1940s. Very little of her work was published, and she died at the age of twenty-nine in 1954, a tragedy that prompted both Margaret Tait and George Mackay Brown to write poems in memoriam. Scott-Moncrieff was a journalist for *The Orcadian* and an author of short stories, children's books and poetry. She died in a tragic drowning incident in 1943 at the age of twenty-nine.

The title of Tait's film *A Pleasant Place* (1969) was taken from Edwin Muir's poem 'To Ann Scott-Moncrieff', in which he quotes Scott-Moncrieff as saying 'the world is a pleasant place'. Scott-Moncrieff was also thought to have inspired the character of Greta, a poet, in Tait's only feature film, *Blue Black Permanent* (1992). Structured over three generations, *Blue Black Permanent* reflects on the circularity of experience from generation to generation. The hall-of-mirrors effect down the generations was echoed in the film's production: in her notebook, Tait praised the resemblance of an auditioning actor to Scott-Moncrieff; *Gerda* Stevenson was eventually cast as *Greta*, and the uncanny resemblance of Gerda to Tait as a younger woman was remarked upon in a letter from Tait's friend Peter Hollander.

By the time Tait released *Blue Black Permanent* in 1992, she was seventy-three years old, a fact that seemed of overriding significance in much of the press's coverage of the film.[17] *Blue Black Permanent* was the culmination of many years' work, the end result

Gerda Stevenson as Greta in Blue Black Permanent. *Courtesy of BFI*

of a script originally titled *Dark Water*, which was based on a novel that Tait had begun in the 1950s. The goal for Tait was always the feature-length film and much of her short work was made with an eye towards developing projects in this direction. Although she did not shrink from commercially led cinema, the development of her filmmaking activity outside commercial frameworks allowed her to develop her own unique vision and approach to filmmaking, which had more in common with the artistry of the lone poet than the collaborative and industry-led approach of a commercial filmmaker.

Tait's Approach to Filmmaking

Tait returned from Italy in the 1950s with the resolute intention of working within the film industry. Later in life she reflected: 'my original interest was in features [...] that is why I went to the Ce Sp di C in Rome in the first place'. While she was in Rome, 'Renoir was shooting *The Golden Coach,* de Sica was working on Centro's own stages, Zampa and Blasetti were regular visitors, and so on.'[18] While Tait did not ascribe wholly to the Neorealist approach, Ancona Films adopted similar working methods, making films on a smaller budget, using real locations and local untrained actors. What Tait encountered on her return to Scotland, however, was an industry led by the successes of the documentary movement under the formidable John Grierson. In 1954, the Films of Scotland committee of which Grierson had been a founding member, was re-established. Initially formed in 1938 by the Scottish Secretary of State and the Scottish Development Council, the committee's remit was to encourage the production of films of 'national interest'.

Grierson showed an interest in Tait's work, but when he offered suggestions for editing it, Tait was not prepared to compromise.[19] Grierson's response is not surprising. As has been argued elsewhere, Grierson under-valued aesthetics in documentary; he also had a lack of regard for Neorealist methods of working.[20] Tait, on the other hand, had very little interest in documentary film-making, explaining that it:

> didn't really attract me very much. I like the idea of making a film equivalent of portrait painting. I did 3Ps of 3 of my friends in Rome [*Three Portrait Sketches* (1951)], and the next year, home in Orkney, I made a portrait of my mother [*A Portrait of Ga* (1952)] [...] I was trying for a sort of formality – a juxtaposition of images related to colour, composition, movement.[21]

According to Tait's notebooks, Grierson did offer Tait work, but only if she was prepared to work according to his rules. If she didn't conform to his methods, Grierson said she would never survive as a filmmaker in Scotland.[22] Tait refers to her troublesome relationship to this period in a dossier on Scottish cinema written in 1998. She writes:

> A 'Scottish Cinema' can only come from what's welling up in people to make. In the dreadful days of the Films of Scotland Committee everybody was expected to turn out the same sort of stuff; and it was awful, friends, and could be no other under the remit people were given.[23]

Instead, Tait opted to work independently, out of necessity. She maintained throughout her life that there was never any film industry in Scotland to which she could have attached her film-making activities, although she had many friends making films in Scotland and there were many whose work she admired over the years, such as Bill Forsyth and Charles Gormley. Her most notable supporters were, perhaps, the filmmakers Murray and Barbara Grigor (the latter was the producer of *Blue Black Permanent*).

In addition to these friends and supporters, there was evidence of occasional support from the Scottish Arts Council. *Land Makar* (1981) was given funding for post-production in 1981, and in 1974, Tait received funding as the first prize winner of the 'Artist as Filmmaker' competition, an award enabling her to make *Colour Poems* (1974). She also experimented with an Orkney film magazine project funded by the Orkney Education Committee. Her film *The Drift Back* (1956), received funding through this route. And, in the 1950s, Tait approached the libraries of Scottish universities with a proposal to fund a film portrait of Hugh MacDiarmid. The appeal was not taken up, but Tait still managed to complete the film in 1964.

It was perhaps outside Scotland that Tait's work made most impact. *Rose Street* (1956) first appeared at the Universal Exhibition in Brussels in 1958 as part of the international experimental film competition and was then shown at several festivals and screenings in Ireland, England and Wales throughout the 1970s and 80s. Most notably, in 1975, Tait's work was selected for inclusion in the First Festival of Independent British Cinema in Bristol and, in 1987, for 'The Elusive Sign: Ten Years of British Avant-Garde', a three-year international tour organised by the British Council. Although two retrospectives of her work have now been held as part of the Edinburgh International Film Festival (one in her lifetime in 1970 and one posthumous in 2004), it is fair to say that most of the interest in hosting screenings of her work has come from outside Scotland.

Tait completed over thirty short films throughout her lifetime, ranging from portraits and abstract animations to concentrated studies of place. She also made what she referred to as 'film poems'. Although definitions of film poems vary (and it could be argued that all of Tait's films could be described as such), it is perhaps the concentrated way of looking in Tait's films that has most in common with other poetic forms. This intense method of looking, inspired by Federico García Lorca's idea of 'stalking the image', was also closely tied to a technique Tait described as 'breathing with the camera.'[24]

The Relationship between Tait's Poetry and Film

Over time, Tait's artistic preoccupations shifted from page to screen. Later in life she recorded, 'I wonder if I'll ever write again. And yet, when it's films, I feel I could go on making films for the rest of my life.'[25] Still, the relationship between writing and filmmaking, literature and film, remained constant and strong throughout her life. Her preoccupations with writing informed her approach to filmmaking, and vice versa. Tait may have been inspired by the filmmakers she encountered in Italy, but she was equally inspired by writers she encountered on the page and in real life. In addition to Lorca, Lowry, Rimbaud, Rilke and Pound, she expressed great admiration for Lawrence. The influence of Lawrence's *Birds, Beasts, Flowers*,[26] which she described as 'piercing', can be found in Tait's collection *origins and elements* (1959), as can that of MacDiarmid's scientific poems. Her background in medicine is also evident in many of the poems' focus on scientific subjects. She used the symbol for a single heartbeat (reproduced on this book's title page) as a sort of signature in much of her work. Her medical background also manifests itself in many of the poems' almost scientific method of close observation, and a preoccupation with darkness and light in both her poetry and her films finds resonance in Emily Dickinson, another poet much loved by Tait. Her poems 'Epiphany', 'Midwinter', and 'Northerner' are good examples of this, in their depiction of the stark contrasts of light and darkness through the changing seasons, as she experienced thoughout her life in Orkney.

Poets also served as direct inspiration and material for her films. For instance, Tait's film *The Leaden Echo and the Golden Echo* (1955) was a filmic interpretation of Gerard Manley Hopkins' poem of the same title. It was the first time Tait had experimented with using a poem as the basis for a film. She came up with the idea after seeing *La Rose et le Réséda* (André Michel, 1947), a film based on the poem of the same title by Louis Aragon. The film, like Tait's later filmic interpretation of *The Leaden Echo,* is structured around a relatively quick and evenly paced succession of shots, many of which are still, which serve as visual equivalents for the words of Aragon's poem. Tait's approach is similar, with the difference that in Michel's film, the words of the poem are reserved for ending of the film; whereas, in Tait's film, the words of Hopkin's poem are spoken throughout, with the images providing a sort of visual translation. Tait described taking 'several years to gather filmed material to match the words of Manley Hopkins' poem on the soundtrack'.[27]

Not surprisingly, Lorca's poetry also features considerably in Tait's films. She even wrote her own translation of *Poet in New York*[28] because she was unhappy with the existing translation. After completing it, she went on to create a series of twenty-nine watercolour illustrations to accompany it.[29] Many years later, Tait continued her exploration of *Poet in New York*, this time in film, including reference to it in her films *Colour Poems* (1974) and *Tailpiece* (1976). (See p. 31 for a still from *Tailpiece* that references Lorca.) Tait writes:

> It's 'Poet In New York' lying on the window-seat in TAILPIECE of course, and some of the words I float through the film are from a translation I made of that book. 'Meanwhile, meanwhile, ah meanwhile', 'A fish swam in the moon', 'Love, love, love' [...] In 'Numen of the Boughs' in COLOUR POEMS 74 I was referring at the same time to a line in that poem and to black and white photographs *I think* I remember seeing, of snipers in trees, frozen dead and still clutching their rifles.[30]

Tait refers here to her poem spoken on the soundtrack of *Colour Poems*. *Colour Poems* and perhaps the film *Orquil Burn* (1955), are examples of films which incorporate her own poetry as part of the soundtrack. In many of her films, the spoken word disappears entirely. For instance, even though her poetry features in the lyrics of the musical soundtrack of *Where I Am Is Here* (1964), she writes:

Still from On the Mountain *(1974), 'Jungle Skins Rule'. Courtesy of Scottish Screen Archive, National Library of Scotland / copyright © Alex Pirie*

The kind of precision which holds 'Where I Am Is Here' together doesn't depend on words: about half a dozen recurring themes – a stone thrown in the water, a car door shutting, traffic, buildings seen from passing buses, and so on – act upon each other, and are then accompanied by Hector MacAndrew's music for my poem 'Hilltop Pibroch'.[31]

In Tait's films, the poetry is evidenced in the image, an approach echoed in her appreciation of Lorca's 'stalking the image'. She explains (quoting Lorca[32]):

'For Gongora, an apple is no less intense than the sea, a bee no less astonishing than a forest. He takes his stand before created Nature with penetrating gaze and admires an identical beauty which equates all forms. He enters what may well be called the universe of each thing and matches his sensibility with the sensations which surround it. For this reason, the apple and the sea evoke the same response; for he knows that the world of the apple is as infinite as the world of the sea.' And so on. 'Gongora treats all materials in the same scale;'... 'The poet must know this', Lorca says.

What I am trying to find, with the help of my camera, is what is behind, say, a scrawled message about 'Jungle Skins Rule', the people who walk up and down, the children playing (but who are no longer there), objects for sale in a shop window, – that is equal – or equally demands attention – in a way that only the motion picture camera has a language for.[33]

Here Tait is calling on the perceived objectivity of the technological aspects of cinema, the camera and its presumed ability to present objects within its frame in great and equal detail, in order to develop what she believes to be a pure form of poetry. It is not surprising then that she disliked the use of cinematic devices such as fades or dissolves which might be seen to interrupt the focused, seemingly objective gaze.

Tait's engagement with Lorca's work in her writing and on film is also evident in her working methods. Films often began life in the pages of Tait's notebook. Lists of places, images or scenes would begin to carve out rough sculptural forms. Eventually, shot lists evolve into a poetic commentary that might be spoken by Tait on the soundtrack. In *Orquil Burn*, for example, Tait includes a shot list of nearly two hundred items, worked on and amended over time, including shots she 'has done' – waterfall at Scapa, field below Orquil; shots she would like 'more of' – Caldale cows, meadowsweet, a small waterfall; and shots she 'must do' – peat, sphagnum moss and cotton. In this sense, the lists are composed to reassess the progress of each project.[34] The lists also form part of the evolution of the film's spoken word soundtrack, sometimes written in essay form, other times in quotations, presumably from other sources such as family and friends ('when there's no wind to turn the windmill, the waterwheel does its work', for example).[35]

Like many of Tait's films, *Orquil Burn* is structured around memory, drawing on a familiarity with a subject, but it is also an exploration of the subject by the camera, which allows for new ways of looking and new discoveries to be made. Tait's camera retraces elements of the landscape familiar from her youth, and although she expects to discover the burn to have an isolated source, she is surprised to find that 'it turned out that the sources were many, the origins widespread'.[36] Her notes on *Orquil Burn* reflect this interplay between the notation of memory and the exploration of the subject in new ways. She recalls how 'water used to meander and get lost in the fields. Uncle Peter had the burn channelled straight for the proper drainage of his lands. The flowers came and grew beside it.'[37] Ultimately, what is left, through this process of development, is the commentary:

There is a burn in the Orkney Isles
Comes tumbling over the Scapa Banks
And enters the sea by a waterfall.

Follow this burn up to its source.
Running water is a useful force –
It can drive a waterwheel,
A waterwheel for machinery
in use at the Scapa Distillery.

This is the burn that used to flow over the fields as it
happened to go.
They changed its course, but the flowers still grow –
Mimulus and meadowsweet –
A recognisable Orkney burn,
The wonderfully useful Orquil Burn.

Over the first stone bridge passes the main road
To Orphir.

A fence across the burn
marks the boundary of Orquil Farm.

In the house of Orquil the Maxwells live.
Jean comes down to feed the chickens.
Tito helps – he's a friendly dog,
A chubby pet and dog of the house.

Uncle Peter – with elderly Spot – farms Orquil.

There are some brown trout in the burn.

The oats in the field by the burn are green,
But filling well.

Over there the windmill is driving a pump to supply
water to the farm of Orquil and the red-roofed
Bungalow and all the farm cottages.
Surprisingly often the wind fails and the
windpump stops
        – so –
The men of the farm are piping water, and leading it
Through a slate-floored cement-roofed little tunnel
And more pipes
And a wooden duct
To a new small waterwheel,
And this system can be turned on to work the pump
On days when there is not enough wind to turn the
windmill.

From the wheel a ditch takes the water back to the burn.

A big milldam was once built to make a really large
Reservoir for the mill wheel. It is rather too big
For the burn, and in any case is now out-dated, by
Modern engines at the mill.
But it does for boys to play in.

An older dam and sluice exist, and are still used,
For the big waterwheel, which used to be the main
Driving force for the threshing mill.
It is still used for some minor machinery on the farm.

Some of the water from the wheel goes into a horse trough.

Most of the mill stream returns to the burn.

Segs are iris leaves, and can be made into seggy boats.

The wind is on the water under the arched bridge

Still from Orquil Burn *(1955). Courtesy of Scottish Screen Archive, National Library of Scotland / copyright © Alex Pirie*

Built like a dyke
Of stones now patterned with lichen plants.

Near this bridge there is a part of the burn which
Used to get called 'the deep bit' by the children.

Above the round-arched bridge, more deep bits.

The shallower stretches were called 'rapids'.

This is the straight channel Uncle Peter had made.
The burn used to wind over the land and lose itself
In marsh and bog.
The straight channel drains the fields and carries
the water down to serve the farm.

The flowers came and grew beside it.

The straight channel is the burn.

A square bridge with two spans crosses it.

The next bridge is a three-span bridge, broken-down and
neglected, at the very outer boundary of Orquil Farm.

The burn is narrow all the way to
The newest, well-made, no-nonsense, severe little
Bridge the Army made, serving the camp there was
Called Caldale Camp.

The Army came and built their huts;
They left their empty tins
And a waste of makeshift desolate hearths to be overgrown.

Down by the burn, another derelict – Tommy Clouston's
Old boat.

The Caldale bridge. This land is Caldale Farm.
That's the farm of Longhouse over there.

Here the burn is bordering Caldale's land.

The sun comes and goes.
Clouds blow away, then cover it again.

Two or three flagstones here make a bridge over the narrow
                                                    burn.

Ragged robin
Meadowsweet.

A drinking place for Caldale's cattle.

And out on the hill, no cattle, no fields.

A sort of ford for the carts which go for the peats.

A wooden plank across a ditch in the heather is
The last of all the bridges.
It leads to the peat banks.

Primitive mares' tail plants grow out of the side
Of this old vegetable deposit, peat.

The water runs away.

The peats are placed on edge to dry.

People from all the houses round about can come
And cut peats on the hill.

The lonely owl is here.

The flowers are very short in the wet hillside.

Water drips from their roots
And runs away to make the Orquil Burn.

The whole hillside is wet.

Wetness from the peat runs off and makes a burn.
It is nearly always windy in Orkney.
The bright plants grow low.

Down below runs the burn, through the heather, the
rushes, the grass, down past the old camp there,
and off towards Orquil Farm and out to the sea at
Scapa.

Tait's exhaustive listing is all part of the rough material with which
she works, further evidence of an unrelenting attention to detail
associated with 'stalking the image'. Further illustration of this
is given in Tait's poem 'Now' and a corresponding diary entry
included in this collection (p. 149), written by Tait in 1949,
describing hours spent trying to capture the opening of a flower
with the varying shutter speeds of her camera. In the end, the
experiment didn't work, but for Tait the process is as important as
what comes out of the process.

When John Grierson viewed Tait's *Orquil Burn*, his advice was
that she should edit it. Tait refused, an action which meant her
work was unlikely to be supported by Grierson, but it was a point
she was unwilling to compromise on. This resistance to compro-
mise meant that Tait held on to what she saw as essential to her
poetry and films, what she refers to as 'folk-poetry or blood-
poetry':

It is the raw material of poetry in Paul Valéry's sense. In the
same way, 'Orquil Burn' is the raw material of a film rather than
a film itself. But that doesn't mean that some busybody of a
Grierson could take it and hash it about – *edit* it and make it into
a tak-tak-tak natty little short film. It isn't *that* kind of raw mate-
rial. It's not just footage. It is a made thing. It is a made thing, set
like that on purpose, but its form is distant or unfinished
perhaps. It is raw material in the sense that working from that
one could now set out and make a real film of Orquil Burn. In
fact I was more correct before when I said my films are sketches
for films rather than films themselves.[38]

In the same passage, she goes on to say: 'The real feat is to have the blood-image and the through-image perfectly united. That is major poetry.'

As the filmmaker Peter Todd suggests, Tait's is 'a way of working [...] people associate with an artist or a composer or somebody rather than a filmmaker'.[39] While a filmmaker might be more 'project-based' and focused on the short term, as Tait argues above, her view was more open, unfolding across the long term.

In her unpublished poem, 'Seeing is Believing and Believing's Seeing', written in 1958, Tait writes:

It's the looking that matters,
The being prepared to see what there is to see.
Staring has to be done:
That I must do.

The poem continues:

The reason I go on living is because I never win.
I lose, and continue.
Success is the end of trying.
Success is defeat.
Success wilts the spirit.
Success is the great discontent.

For Tait, this engagement with the continual evolution of her work was important. The emphasis on raw material over the finished, polished and complete, allowed Tait to approach her subjects with an openness that resisted forcing them into preconceived formats. Her contempt for conventions in general – societal, generic and otherwise – is evident throughout her films, poetry, writing and short stories. Most of her poems are written in free verse and are conversational in tone; as in her filmmaking, she allows room for ideas to develop and breathe. 'One World, One Sun' (p. 72) is generously structured like an unfolding mindscape, scouring through memories of places Tait has lived – Jhansi, Italy and back to the north – framing them through a consideration of their relationship to the sun. In an untitled poem from *origins and elements*, she urges poetry to 'express the doubt':

Even express the confusion so long as what you see or
half-see with your earth-vision is right there in the
thing.

Tait's favouring of uncertainty over certainty, and her dislike of

Poems, Stories and Writings

approaches which follow established conventions, is also evident in other writings. Two of the short stories in this collection, 'The Incomers' and 'The Song Gatherer' (pp. 131, 136), focus on their characters' misguided struggles to contain or record Orkney's cultural and natural heritage. The characters' depiction echoes Tait's misgivings about documentary's ability to represent reality meaningfully. In her essay on the film poem (p. 166), she writes:

> The contradictory or paradoxical thing is that in a *Documentary* the real things depicted are liable to lose their reality by being photographed and presented in that 'documentary' way, and there's no poetry in that.

Tait is interested in an emotional truth, in looking closely at things that can be 'brought into the imaginary whole along with their own actuality'.[40]

Edinburgh in the 1950s and 1960s

In 1954, the year she returned from Rome, Tait held the first 'Rose Street Film Festival' at the studio she established for Ancona Films at 91 Rose Street. The informal event provided the opportunity to screen her own work alongside the work of her fellow students from the Centro Sperimentale. Invitations were sent to writers, artists and filmmakers such as Edwin Muir, Stanley Cursiter, Eric Linklater, Compton Mackenzie, John Grierson and Forsyth Hardy and, as with all the screenings held by Tait, participation was encouraged from the local community. In an interview, Alex Pirie recalls enlisting the vocal skills of his son to shout from the first floor window, 'Exhibition!', while a fresh pot of coffee was brewed to entice potential audience members up the stairs.[41] After the festival, a review in an Edinburgh paper noted the attendance of John Grierson, who was recorded as saying, 'Fantastic, I haven't seen anything so beautiful for a long time.'[42]

A second Rose Street Film Festival was held in 1955, continuing the previous year's approach by exhibiting Tait's own work alongside three films from other filmmakers from Rome. The events were emblematic of the Tait's commitment to establishing a vibrant community of filmmakers, similar to what she had experienced in Rome.

Tait held tenancy of the studio space until 1973, residing there from 1954 to the early 1960s, when she moved first to Sutherland before returning to Orkney as a permanent resident in 1968. At the time, Rose Street was a meeting-place for the group now known as the Rose Street Poets, including Sydney Goodsir Smith, Hugh MacDiarmid, Norman MacCaig and Tom Scott. Although Tait was friends and acquaintances with a number of poets and met with them on various occasions, as Alex Pirie recalled, she was never a real pub-goer and only occasionally went along to the pubs that the activities of the poetry scene centered on. It may also be that Tait did not feel entirely comfortable or confident with the scene. In one notebook, describing a meeting taking place with a group of Glasgow poets, she writes, 'All very nice and Milne's bar ish and Abbotsfordish. But I'm not up to it at present, not equal to it.'[43] The Rose Street poetry scene was largely a masculine environment. In her biography of George Mackay Brown, Maggie Fergusson considers the effects of this in relation to Tait's acquaintance Stella Cartwright. Cartwright played a starring role in Tait's film *Palindrome* (1964). Although they were never close friends, Alex Pirie described Cartwright as having a sort of 'European sensibility' that would have appealed to Tait and a 'real energy' that Tait adeptly captures on film. Cartwright had been introduced to the Rose Street pubs at the age of sixteen by her father. Known as the 'Muse of Rose Street', she had a number of affairs with poets asso-

Stella Cartwright in Palindrome. *Courtesy of Scottish Screen Archive, National Library of Scotland / copyright © Alex Pirie*

Poems, Stories and Writings

ciated with the scene. Fergusson wonders whether Cartwright's own unrealised potential as a poet might have benefited from the support and guidance of an established female poet.[44]

Tait held similar reservations in relation to the filmmaking community and was reluctant to attend 'events'. Even before she returned to Orkney, she was largely working independently. In one notebook entry, written in 1958, Tait describes receiving the 35mm prints of *Calypso* (1955) and then arranging to see them one morning on her own in a local cinema.[45] Neither in Edinburgh nor in Orkney was there a community of filmmakers with which Tait could work, equivalent to that she had encountered in Rome.

Tait and Pirie's closest friends on Rose Street were Kulgin Duval and Edward Nairn, dealers in rare books who lived across the street from Ancona Films. It is likely that it was Duval and Nairn who introduced Tait to Hugh MacDiarmid. In the early 1960s they were interested in publishing MacDiarmid's collected work,[46] and Tait occasionally accompanied them on visits to MacDiarmid and his wife Valda at Brownsbank Cottage just outside Biggar, in Lanarkshire. There is one particularly vivid account of such a visit in a letter to Alex Pirie in March 1962:

Last Friday morning leaving shortly after 8, I drove Kulgin down to MacDiarmid's with Michael Peto to photograph MacD with that young Russian poet Yevtushenko. I had already driven him down the day before to see if it was all right. The Russians were very fine, very remarkable. He comes from a town called *Winter* in Siberia. The girl too very beautiful, but ill, finding it almost unbearably painful to walk because of an abscess 'down below' as Valda put it, and yet very much present. See the carnation MacD has in his buttonhole looking as if it was growing out of a glass of beer – the counterpart is here in a jug on the yellow chest of drawers. So what was this visit. Michael Peto taking 150 photos. MacDiarmid saying quite a lot of rubbish. The Russians bewildered by some of his party line point of view, very far from their own way of expressing themselves. Well not party line exactly but politically-framed opinions like – Eliot – he went fascist in the end, they all go fascist in the end, Eliot, Yeats, they all do. Valda was wearing a CND badge, showed it proudly to the girl; it meant nothing to her. 'Ban the Bomb,' explained Valda. 'Bomb?' – very puzzled. 'Ban,' said Valda, '*ban* – ban the bomb.' But the girl just repeated 'bomb?' shaking her head at her own inability to follow the

English. Neither of them spoke English but there was a very good interpreter, and they could understand some tho not all of what was said in English tho unable to reply in the same language.

This entry, written the same year that Tait began work on her film portrait of MacDiarmid, illustrates how, although they were never close friends, Tait's relationship and correspondence with Valda and MacDiarmid had an stimulating effect. MacDiarmid also published some of Tait's poetry in the magazine he was editing in the 1950s, *The Voice of Scotland*.

Tait's work was also supported by the artist and gallery-owner Richard Demarco, who hosted a number of readings and screenings of Tait's work. In 1972, for instance, Tait read alongside Robert Garioch and Edwin Morgan – Morgan had reviewed her book *origins and elements* for *New Saltire* in 1961.[47] In a letter to Sean Connery written around the same time as the reading, Richard Demarco writes, 'You know already how highly I regard Margaret Tait and her work. She is a classic example of a first class Scot living here and being ignored, with something significant to say to the whole world about Scotland.'[48]

Robert Garioch, Edwin Morgan and Margaret Tait,
Richard Demarco Gallery, Edinburgh Arts, 1972.
Courtesy of The Richard Demarco Gallery Digital Archives

Poems, Stories and Writings

Tait's Legacy as Writer and Filmmaker

In her essay on Tait in the *Margaret Tait Reader* published by LUX in 2004, Ali Smith asks:

> Why are there no poems by Margaret Tait included in the (most definitive so far) volume of *Modern Scottish Women Poets* published by Canongate in 2003? Why, when you ask most literate film and book lovers, including people in Scotland, even in the north of Scotland, have they heard of Margaret Tait, do they look distant and shake their heads? Why did I, as a reasonably well-read Highlander myself, a person who grew up in the Highlands and studied Scottish literature alongside other literatures, and as someone who has been seeking out all sorts of genres and books and all sorts of genres of films and art all my life, only come across my first Margaret Tait poems and films as recently as two or three years ago?

Smith ends her questioning with a plea: 'Someone should publish a Collected Tait, illustrated with stills from her films.'[49] This is essentially what LUX's Tait reader achieved, publishing essays, reproducing material from the archive, including some of her poetry and short stories. And this present collection, by focusing on Tait's writing, hopes to continue this effort.

*

It is unfortunate that Tait's work was not more recognised in her own lifetime. However, Tait was not always comfortable with efforts made to promote her work and she certainly was not comfortable with the promotion of herself as the focus of attention. During her lifetime Tait was the subject of two television profiles, one a thirty-minute programme for BBC Scotland in 1979, and the other a thirty-five-minute programme for Channel 4 and the Arts Council of Great Britain in 1983. Although Channel 4 followed the 1983 documentary with a broadcast of her film *Where I Am is Here* and in 1987 screened a selection of her films as part of the Eleventh Hour series, the earlier BBC Scotland documentary relied solely on extracts. Tait was resistant to the use of extracts in the profiles and voiced concerns that people would assume that what they were seeing were the actual films. Both programmes undoubtedly increased the visibility of her work, but even so she was very outspoken in her dislike of them. She had been intensely involved in the creation of their scripts, with each production involving a series of letters relating to the accuracy of biographical details and the text for the interviews, yet she felt that there was too much emphasis on her and not enough on her films.

This experience left her wary of accepting future requests. Even a proposal from her friend, the photographer Gunnie Moberg, in 1994, to photograph Tait for an exhibition on Scottish writers and filmmakers, was turned down in a letter from Tait explaining how it was the 'wrong side of the camera' for her.[50] However, Gunnie Moberg was eventually successful in taking one of the few photographs of the filmmaker.[51]

In spite of the profiles, screenings of Tait's films were still quite rare. Certainly her decision to enter a few of her films into distribution with the London Film-Makers' Co-op in 1979[52] helped to create greater circulation of her work, but throughout her life she remained reluctant to focus any significant attention on its preservation and exhibition. Still, it is difficult to be completely sure of Tait's feelings in relation to her own legacy. Her words are often contradictory in many respects; her actions too. She kept highly detailed catalogue notes describing the contents and condition of her film holdings. In one of her notebooks she describes a day's activity sorting through her film stock and cleaning a few films that she thinks look in particular need of care.[53] On one hand, this could be interpreted as a filmmaker with an eye to preserving her work for the future, on the other, it could be read as Tait maintaining the condition of stock that she might desire to use for future film work – she often considered prospects for future films by working through film material that had yet to be incorporated into previous work. She also had a tendency to accumulate material over a number of years before incorporating it into a film. In many respects, her lack of interest in the final film and what would happen to it, was probably because for her, each film was more to do with an exploration of process.

Although Tait worked in a wholly professional manner in the production of her films, she did not have the same interest in their promotion and distribution. Instead, it was friends or artists whose enthusiasm compelled them to share her work with others that drew her work to the attention of wider audiences. This is the case with many of the screenings organised in England by Mike Leggett. In later years filmmakers such as Ute Aurand in Berlin and Peter Todd in London were keen advocates of Tait's films, with Todd including Tait's work in a film programme that he

Portrait of Margaret Tait by Gunnie Moberg.
Courtesy of the Orkney Archive / copyright © Tam MacPhail

curated on film poems and Aurand organising a number of screen-ings in Berlin, eventually purchasing her own 16mm copies for this purpose. Aurand, in a letter to Tait, also confessed to going against Tait's wishes by videoing some of Tait's work to show to the

American filmmaker, writer and archivist Jonas Mekas when she visited him in New York in 1994. [54]

The restoration of her films by the Scottish Screen Archive, LUX and Peter Todd and the subsequent touring exhibition ensures that Tait's work is preserved and will have a longevity beyond her lifetime. In addition to the major retrospective at the Edinburgh International Film Festival in 2004, the touring film programme travelled to over nine countries and three continents. Today, the filmmaker's work is regularly exhibited and a new award for artist filmmakers in Scotland – the Glasgow Film Festival Margaret Tait Award (supported by Creative Scotland and LUX) – gives due recognition to Tait's pioneering role in experimental filmmaking in Scotland, while also ensuring the kind of support for artists that was lacking throughout Tait's lifetime.

Tait's films are available through the Scottish Screen Archive and LUX. Both have comprehensive websites with a few films available for online viewing, and LUX also offers a DVD featuring a selection of her films. These new possibilities for viewing her work have undoubtedly increased the number of informal screenings of Tait's work and made it more widely accessible. Tait, more than likely, would have approved. She may have been against the use of her works in extracted form for documentary or television programmes, but she was a strong advocate for the screening of work in unlikely locations. She organised screenings at the Phoenix cinema in Kirkwall, but she also toured around the smaller Orkney islands, screening her films in village halls and other venues. She was known to project films on the wall of her sitting room for visiting friends and family. Although the diminishing effects of YouTube transmission may worry some admirers of Tait's films, the democratic nature of new distribution technologies is something that I think would have appealed to Tait, who would have advocated anything that would enable people to organise their own screenings, in their own homes or other venues, to generally get involved and to engage with the making and exhibiting of films.

The recent successes in relation to the preservation and exhibition of Tait's films are cause for celebration, but it is also dismaying that despite the increased visibility of her achievements in recent years, her work is in many ways still neglected in terms of both recognition and preservation. Even after the publication of the LUX *Margaret Tait Reader* and Ali Smith's inclusion of two of Tait's poems in her anthology *The Reader* (Constable, 2006), recent editions of Canongate's *Modern Scottish Women Poets* have continued to overlook Tait and, as mentioned on p. 5, a history of Orcadian literature published in 2010 omits any mention of Tait's writing.

The screening of Tait's films in recent years has, though, begun to resonate in the work of contemporary artists. In 2011 Tacita Dean exhibited a celebration and homage to analogue filmmaking in the Turbine Hall of the Tate Modern. Tait's name was referenced several times by contributors to the accompanying catalogue and website.

Tait's archive, both paper and film, is vast; a fact that makes it extraordinary, but also challenging as regards preservation. Much work has been done, but there is much still to do. It is important that the energy and enthusiasm for Tait's work is sustained and underpinned by serious efforts to preserve her films.

While Tait is increasingly cited as an influence by contemporary artists, because of the lack of attention that has been given to her writing, similar claims cannot be made in relation to contemporary writing. It is hoped that this collection will enable such connections to begin to be made.

A Note on the Text

As the availability of Tait's work grows (even if sometimes at a frustratingly slow pace), so does the amount of literature written about her. For a full bibliography of resources relating to Margaret Tait see pp. 171–6, below. The most comprehensive of these is *Subjects and Sequences: A Reader*, edited by Peter Todd and Ben Cook, published by LUX in 2004. The Reader contains essays by a range of contributors, from Ali Smith to the artist, curator and academic Lucy Reynolds and film archivists Janet McBain and Alan Russell. The variety of sources allows for a rich understanding of the collection, restoration and interpretations of Tait's films and poetry. The book also reproduces materials from the archive, some of Tait's poetry, writings and a short story, and offers an extensive and useful list of resources.

Most of the poetry gathered here is from three collections: *Subjects and Sequences* (1960), *origins and elements* (1959) and *The Hen and the Bees* (1960). Tait described the first as 'the most musical', the second as 'the most thoughtful' and the latter as 'the most ficticious (or fictional, should I say)'. *The Hen and the Bees* was also felt by Tait to be the most closely tied to her Orcadian roots because of the poems' mode of storytelling. It also contains a sequence of poems on queens, devised by Tait as a 'riposte' to a series of paintings of kings by Robin Philipson, a lecturer at Edinburgh College of Art at the time. Tait initially attempted to respond in painting herself, but then *'wrote* the painting instead'.[55] Most of the poetry was written in a concentrated period of time, largely the late 1950s and early 1960s. Unpublished and/or uncollected poems, writings and short stories are also included. Although it may seem that later in life Tait almost wholly traded in her pen for her camera, the images contained within the earlier written work can be seen to resonate in the powerful poetry composed on screen throughout her career as a filmmaker.

For the most part, editorial interventions have been kept to a minimum throughout the collection. The only minor amendments have been to replace older hyphenated forms of words like 'to-day' and 'to-night' to reflect modern conventions. Dates of first publication have been included in brackets after any works that were previously published and, where known, the date of composition has also been included. Previously published items are noted and dates included where possible.

Notes

1 'Films of Margaret Tait', film programme, Calton Studios, 6 May 1979, Margaret Tait collection, Orkney Archive, D97/25.
2 Hugh MacDiarmid, 'Intimate Film Making in Scotland: The Work of Dr Margaret Tait', *Scottish Field*, October 1960, reprinted in Angus Calder, Glen Murray and Alan Riach (eds.), *Hugh MacDiarmid: The Raucle Tongue*, vol. III (Manchester: Carcanet, 1998), pp. 415–17: 417.
3 *origins and elements*, poems (Edinburgh: M.C. Tait, 1959); *The Hen and the Bees: Legends and Lyrics*, poems (Edinburgh: M.C. Tait, 1960); *Subjects and Sequences*, poems (Edinburgh: M.C. Tait, 1960); *Lane Furniture: A Book of Stories* (Edinburgh: M.C. Tait, 1959); *The Grassy Stories: Short Stories for Children* (Edinburgh: M.C. Tait, 1959).
4 Notes for television profile, Margaret Tait collection, Orkney Archive, D97/1/2.
5 The article was never published.
6 Pirie was also a writer. His poetry can be found in *Lines Review*, no. 15, Summer 1959.
7 Letter to Alex Pirie, 28 November 1960.
8 'George Mackay Brown Remembered', *Chapman*, no. 84, 1996, pp. 33–4.
9 Tait notebook, December 1958.
10 Kulgin Duval, a bookseller, a friend of Tait and Pirie. (See p. 21.)
11 Letter to Alex Pirie, 21 May 1960.
12 Robert Rendall, *The Orkney Shore* (Kirkwall: W.R. Mackintosh, 1973).
13 Simon Hall, *The History of Orkney Literature* (Edinburgh: John Donald, 2010).
14 In a letter to Ernest Marwick, 24 April 1958, Tait recalls Allison's fondness for

her poem 'Pomona' and its reference to 'Holly Cottage, Windlesham' where they had both stayed (Orkney Archive, D31/60/4). There is also mention of Leonard Tait's feedback during Tait's editing process in Tait's notebooks, April 1952.

15 Ernest Marwick, *An Anthology of Orkney Verse* (Kirkwall: The Kirkwall Press, 1949). Work by Scott-Moncrieff has appeared in other poetry anthologies such as Catherine Kerrigan's *An Anthology of Women Poets* (Edinburgh: Edinburgh University Press, 1991). There was also a special issue of the Scottish literary magazine *Chapman* (no. 38, 1984) which featured previously unpublished work by Scott-Moncrieff.

16 Unpublished poem, Ernest W. Marwick papers, Orkney Archive, D31/39/6.

17 See, for instance, 'Mags, 73, in Blue Movie!', *Scottish Sun*, 4 June 1992.

18 Tait notebook, 1986, pp. 52–3. This is from a significant collection of Tait's notebooks which will be added to the collection in the Orkney archive in 2012.

19 For more detail on this see Sarah Neely, '"Ploughing a lonely furrow": Margaret Tait and "professional" filmmaking practices in 1950s Scotland', in Ian Craven (ed.), *Movies on Home Ground: Explorations in Amateur Cinema* (Newcastle: Cambridge Scholars Press, 2010), pp. 301–26.

20 Ian Aitken, *The Documentary Film Movement: an Anthology* (Edinburgh: Edinburgh University Press, 1998), p. 59.

21 Notes for television profile, Margaret Tait collection, Orkney Archive, D97/1/2.

22 Tait notebook, April 1958, p. 14.

23 Tait, Margaret, statement on six films selected by filmmaker as 'models for a representation of Scotland on screen', in Kenny Mathieson (ed.), *Desperately Seeking Cinema?*, Glasgow Film Theatre, May–October 1988, pp. 83–4.

24 Tamara Krikorian, '"On the Mountain" and "Land Makar": Landscape and Townscape in Margaret Tait's work', in Michael Maziere and Nina Danino (eds.), *The Undercut Reader: Critical Writings on Artists' Film and Video* (London: Wallflower, 2002), pp. 103–5: 103.

25 Tait notebook, 1958. Tait's sentiments have much in common with those of the filmmaker and poet Maya Deren. Describing her frustrations with her earlier efforts at written poetry and the difficulty of expressing what was 'essentially a visual experience', Deren said, 'When I got a camera in my hands it was like coming home' (documentary, *In the Mirror of Maya Deren* [Kudláček, 2002]).

26 D.H. Lawrence, *Birds, Beasts and Flowers* (London: Martin Secker, 1923).

27 Notes, Margaret Tait collection, Orkney Archive, D97/37.

28 Federico García Lorca, *Poet in New York* (1940), trans. Ben Belitt (New York: Grove, 1955).

29 These were exhibited at the Kirkwall Library in March 1962 and again in 1964, at Tait's studio in Rose Street, during the Edinburgh Festival.

30 Letter to Ramon Font, 1 July 1993, Margaret Tait collection, Orkney Archive, D97/27.

31 Notes for London Film-Makers' Co-op screening, 'The Films of Margaret Tait', Margaret Tait collection, Orkney Archive, D97/37.

32 Federico García Lorca, 'The Poetic Image of Don Luis de Gongora', *Deep Song and Other Prose* (London and New York: Marion Boyars, 1982), pp. 59–85.

33 Notes for television profile, Margaret Tait collection, Orkney Archive, D97/1/2.

34 Margaret Tait collection, Orkney Archive, D97/3.

35 Notes on *Orquil Burn*, Margaret Tait collection, Orkney Archive, D97/3.

36 Peter Todd and Benjamin Cook (eds.), *Subjects and Sequences: A Margaret Tait*

Reader (London: LUX, 2004), p. 159.

37 Notes on *Orquil Burn*, Margaret Tait collection, Orkney Archive, D97/3.

38 'Personae', unpublished manuscript, Margaret Tait collection, Orkney Archive, D97/32., p. 63.

39 Interview with Peter Todd, 9 April 2011.

40 'Film-poem or Poem-film : A few notes about film and poetry from Margaret Tait', p. 166 below.

41 Interview with Alex Pirie, 1 September 2006.

42 'Orcadian's Film for Edinburgh Festival?', *The Orkney Herald*, 25 July 1957, p. 4.

43 Tait notebooks, October 1958, p. 37.

44 Maggie Fergusson, *George Mackay Brown: The Life* (London: John Murray, 2006).

45 Tait Notebook, October 1958.

46 Hugh MacDiarmid, *The Kind of Poetry I Want* (Edinburgh: K.D. Duval, 1961).

47 Edwin Morgan, 'Who Will Publish Scottish Poetry', review of *origins and elements*, *New Saltire* 2, November 1961, pp. 51–6.

48 Richard Demarco to Sean Connery, 18 October 1972, Margaret Tait Collection, Orkney Archive, D97/15/14/2.

49 Ali Smith, 'The Margaret Tait Years', in Todd and Cook (eds.), *Subjects and Sequences*, pp. 7–27.

50 Letter to Gunnie Moberg, 9 February 1994, Margaret Tait collection, Orkney Archive, D97/1/6.

51 The photograph appears in Gunnie Moberg's *Orkney (Images of Scotland)*, (Edinburgh: Birlinn, 2006).

52 The films included were *Aerial* (1974), *Colour Poems* (1974), *Place of Work* (1976) and *Tailpiece* (1976). Later, *Hugh MacDiarmid, A Portrait* (1964) and *Land Makar* (1981) were added (luxonline.org.uk).

53 Tait notebooks, January to June 1990.

54 Letter from Ute Aurand, 12 June 1994, Margaret Tait collection, Orkney Archive, D97/36.

55 Letter to Ernest Marwick, Orkney Archive, D31/60/4. Robin Philipson designed the cover for Tait's book.

POEMS

Previous page: Still from Tailpiece *(1976). Copyright © Alex Pirie*

from
origins and elements (1959)

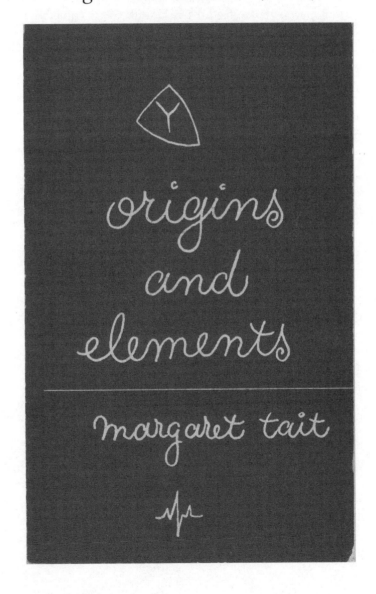

Elasticity

Think of the word, elastic.
The real elastic quality is the being able to spring back
    to the original shape,
Not the being able to be stretched.
So, metal is described as elastic
And steel is the most elastic of all metals.
It is specially manufactured to have the elastic quality
    of retaining its own shape.
Steel is so elastic you can't budge it.

Reading about Rimbaud

Hell consists in a sense of having sinned.
The idea of sin is the actuality of hell.
That's all hell is,
And sure it's plenty.

The heaven within us
Could be, equally, the sense of our own essential
    innocence,
Intuitive sense of animal complexity
Causing our inexplicable behaviour.

'It's a mistake to write a poem that seems more certain'

It's a mistake to write a poem that seems more certain
    of a policy or a belief or anything than you really
    are.
Express the doubt too.
Even express the confusion so long as what you see or
    half-see with your earth-vision is right there in the
    thing.

Emily

Emily Dickinson shut herself in a room
And wrote about her pain.
She wrote too about joy.

Water

Water is an element in one sense but not in the other.
Chemically, it is a compound
H_2O
Two atoms of hydrogen to one of oxygen.
Can you believe it?
Gases,
And they make that stuff!
Light, lightest of all the gases,
Of all the elements, in fact, –
Hydrogen,
Light and explosive.
And oxygen.
Business-like, useful oxygen,
Combustible,
Ready to combine with almost anything.
I've always liked oxygen.
Oxygen.
　Orkney.
　　Ozone.
The air we breathe,
Oxyhaemoglobin,
Life-blood,
And it combines with that light explosive
　　of a hydrogen
And makes –
Water, dammit!
Waters of the world.
You can build an igloo with it.

from *origins and elements* (1959)　　　　　35

Carbon

Carbon
Is diamonds
And it's what we use in the grate or the gas-jet to
warm ourselves by, making it combine with the
oxygen of the air,
Warm combustible oxygen.
There's a flame,
Warmth
And carbon dioxide.
That's all that's left of the carbon
– a whiff.
And carbon
Is one of the essential elements of all living things.
All organic matter
Contains carbon.
It's the scientific definition of an 'organic' substance
that it contains carbon.
Diamonds in the blood,
Coal in the brain-paths,
Heart, muscle, vessels, connective tissue, blood,
lymph, alveoli of the lungs
Ultimately made of protoplasm formed partly of the
life-belonging element, carbon.
Burning it in our bodies makes us warm too,
Turning it into carbon dioxide that we dispose of then
through our lungs into the air.

That black inert-looking element, carbon!
But think of all the things it can do.
It's in rose petals
And tree trunks
And toads,
Imprisoned in compounds represented by those
alarming diagrams which seem so far removed
from reality,
Rings, chains, groups,
Para-
Di-ethyl-tri-benzy-
Names all with a significance relating to the number of
carbon atoms grouped together.
Atom with a solid valency of four

And just occasionally two,
Yet as varied and adaptable as a live thing,
The most varied and adaptable of all elements
As of course is necessary for the one which is to be in
    all living material.
That means, too, all material which has ever been
    living,
Like coal,
Like diamonds.
And it gets into the organic compounds too –
'Organic' because they have carbon in them –
The alkaloids, and the latest medicines devised in the
    laboratory
And synthetic things to wear or make tools of,
The complex compound things with long many-
    hyphened names which are one long cipher quite
    readable by a chemist who has worked among
    those significances,
Containing, all of them, this one black atom in one or
    other of its innumerable manifestations,
Usually along with hydrogen and oxygen
And just one or two other elements to give spice,
    uniqueness, point to the already great variety.
The animal body is almost entirely made of hydrogen
    oxygen and carbon
And nitrogen,
And traces, as they say in chemistry,
Of other things.
After death, the animal body turns into di-hydrogen
    oxide, that is water, and ammonia, and carbon
    dioxide, an inert gas normally present in the air
    anyway.
(Where did it come from?
From the innumerable decomposing animal and
    vegetable bodies?)
We breathe it in and we breathe it out.
It stimulates us by reflex action to breathe deeper
And then we breathe out even more of it, the waste
    product of burning up the carbon in all the cells
    of our bodies,
Carbon, black inert carbon,
Life-belonging carbon.

from *origins and elements* (1959)   37

Reputation

The fairies, the bitches, didn't build the Pyramids;
It was the Pharaohs, the buggers,
As the colonel discovered
In my uncle's joke.
And the fame of little Moses in the basket
Is perceived by some slightly different part of us from
    the part that knows the famous ten
    commandments
Which he wrote on stone
In later life.
In those days in the basket Moses wasn't thinking of
    stone-engraven laws.
He was crying
Because he was hungry.
Hungry for breast-milk was little Moses and he had
    been denied it,
Left in a sweet little basket among the rushes,
Little basket,
Moses.
He never forgot it,
Never forgave it
And went on proving his near-omnipotence for all of
    his life.
So as not to say he was omnipotent exactly
He put it all in the name of God.
God could be omnipotent
– People accept that –
And Moses, wee Moses, the basket, could be his
    Spokesman.
See?
Easy!
Ah well, it's not as easy as all that.
It wouldn't have worked if he hadn't believed it
    himself,
Believed that the One individual God of all the
    universe
Selected him, Moses,
To tell the folks down below
All the news
Of what Heaven expected them to do.

So he wrote it down
And intoned it,
Preached and practised to them as hard as ever he
    could.

Storms

I wished for a storm to test my strength against.
I cried for the gale-force wind,
For electric explosions,
For sheets of rain.
I looked to the motionless wisps of cloud,
To the serene blue of the sky
And wished them transformed.
I wished to be battered and to emerge triumphant.
I love the beating heat of the uncovered sun
And the magic stillness of a wet evening after rain
And a calm of the sea which makes it look like heavy
    Melted deep-coloured stuff;
But, meantime, through it all,
I crave the wave beating
Lashing the untamed earth I live on
And the screaming of the wild atmosphere I live in.
The violence of it pumps my blood faster.

A Fire

The tiniest twigs will nearly always light,
Even if they're wet,
And then, when they're going properly,
Add the slightly bigger ones.
As the flame rises
It will dry off the more sizable sticks you've gathered,
And once the fire is going well
It will burn almost anything,
Except of course the sodden solid masses of old rotten
    log.
Tending a fire

As a full-time occupation
Is a feminine contentment.
To watch the flames rise,
Hear the crackle
And judge the correct moment and the correct place
    to add the next bit of fuel
Satisfies
Some ancient impulse.
Hearth-keeper,
I build a little flame
And keep it there, feed it, keep it going
To warm you all by and feed you and cheer you by
And cheer myself too,
Cheer the deepest comfortless dark in my own self.

Published in *The Voice of Scotland,* vol. 9, no. 1, 1958

Flood-water

Flood-water came out of the sky
As snow.
It blocked the roads and made the surface slippery
By freezing,
And then it turned to rain,
Melted all the hard stuff into mush.
Great lumps of melting snow stuck in the fields,
Made treacherous pools far too near to the houses
And great splashy quagmires in all the roadways.
Wet drowned the little birds.
They shivered to death with their feathers all drookit.
Water stood in the low places and the continual rain
    replenished it.
We feared another flood.
But the miracle always comes;
The rain stops,
The water slowly evaporates and drains away once
    more,
Runs downward to the sea,
Leaving behind a thorough soaking for all of earth's
    surface,

Some of which, alas, it carries away in the rivers and
    into the salt ocean.
But the sun dries the rest,
Warms the generating seed
Which then sends out little rootlets to suck in that
    useful water all around.
In the end it's said to be all for the good
Even if some were drowned,
Even if some were lost.
It seems to be in the long run positive and productive
    even with all that destruction.

Sleep

Sleep
Joins us all.
Sleep
Is what we come out of,
What we return to.
Deep
In our consciousness
Is the great linking thing, sleep.
Just *one* consciousness, the Brahmins say,
One for all of us
And we all dip into it like the porridge-pot in the
    middle of the table,
Select our spoonfuls
But dream of the rest.
The rest is ours too, really,
Or we are its,
All living with little bits of the one huge consciousness
    thrust into us like the processes of the amoeba
    poking out and filling with particles of the parent
    protoplasm.

from *origins and elements* (1959)   41

'Protected in my little house'

Protected in my little house,
I watch the weather.
How it beats at my window-panes!
How it shakes my timbers!
How it howls!
Human beings can make themselves these protective
    boxes
And lie snugly watching what goes on.

To Anybody at All

I didn't want you cosy and neat and limited.
I didn't want you to be understandable,
Understood.
I wanted you to stay mad and limitless,
Neither bound to me nor bound to anyone else's or
    your own preconceived idea of yourself.

Singularity

To be I
Not we
Is the last
And first terrifying demand
Which of a poet is demanded first and last and in the
    middle.

Four or Ninety or ∞ or what

The earth to stand on and to eat,
The water to drink and to wash with,
The air to breathe and to move through,
The fire to warm us
    And to light us,

To take us into the beyond,
Into the world of imagination
– Those four, it was decided by some thinkers long
        ago,
Are elemental to us.
Since then, other thinkers
Have worked out the atomic table.
These are the elements, they say.
Oh, we admit there may be others, yet to be
        discovered,
To fill in those blank spaces we've left,
But fundamentally
This is it.

Einstein meant his theory of relativity
Mathematically
– Or we who talk about it say he did –
But Lawrence too had a theory about relativity,
Or about relatedness,
Not so mathematical
– Or at least not belonging to a separate
        construction called Mathematics –
And if we were to listen carefully to them both
We might hear something
To our advantage, as the lawyers say.
A bequest.
Let us relate the relatedness of Lawrence to the
        relativity of Einstein, we the relatives receiving
        the bequest.

(14 March 1958)

Now

I used to lie in wait to see the clover open
Or close,
But never saw it.
I was too impatient,
Or the movement is too subtle,
Imperceptible

And more than momentary.
My five-year-old self would tire of waiting
And when I looked again
– All closed for the night!
I missed it
Once more.

Cinematographically
I have registered the opening of escholtzia
On an early summer morning.
It gave me a sharp awareness of time passing,
Of exact qualities and values in the light,
But I didn't see the movement
As movement.
I didn't with my own direct perception see the petals
     moving.
Later, on the film, they seemed to open swiftly,
But, at the time,
Although I stared
And felt time not so much moving as being moved in
And felt
A unity of time and place with other times and places
Yet
I didn't see the petals moving.
I didn't see them opening.
They were closed,
And later they were open,
And in between I noted many phases,
But I didn't see them moving open.
My timing and my rhythm could not observe the
     rhythm of their opening.

The thing about poetry is you have to keep doing it.
People have to keep making it.
The old stuff is no use
Once it's old.
It comes out of the instant
And lasts for an instant.
    Take it now
    Quickly
    Without water.

There!

Tomorrow they'll be something else.

Published in *The Voice of Scotland*, vol. 9, no. 1, 1958

Lezione di Recitazione

Beware of approximations,
Tamberlani said to the student actors,
And I was listening.
Again and again he made that point.
Go to the heart of what it is,
Examine each character, each situation, for itself
Each time
And never take the time before's presentation,
Another person's reading
Or anything else that doesn't come out of this, now,
    here.
Read the real individual reason.
Don't approximate
By copying readymade externalisations.

'"Don't meet," they say to me'

'Don't meet,' they say to me.
'Don't get involved.'
But I have to meet
Everyone
And everything.
It isn't a choice. I have to.
'Stay lonely,' they say. 'That's the best.
Be alone.'
But they don't stay alone themselves.
They snuggle in
With several counterpanes
And cups of tea
Provided for them against their loneliness.
It seems to be only me they want to be lonely.

from *origins and elements* (1959)   45

The Unbreakable-Up

Sometimes, when you give a thing a name it recedes.
Other times, no,
It comes all the closer.

I was wondering about things like electrons,
For, with names or without names,
They are almost inconceivable.
I mean they seem like abstract concepts
Although
They are the very source and being of matter, –
If they exist at all.
If there's such a thing as them
They are material things.
It's as difficult to imagine them
As to see the rose close for the night.
That happens on a different scale of time
And electrons, even atoms, are on a different scale of
    size.
Our only aid to seeing that time-rhythm
Is by stop-motion cinematography;
And the microscope enlarges,
  In a sense,
Makes visible, anyway, to our eyes
Things of a size beyond us.
But the scale goes then.
We have no relationship with those huge amoebae
  photographed and filling half a page
Nor with the stained cocci
  Shown as Gram-positive chains.
What has 'Gram' to do with them?
Dark-blue chains of hyphens is not what they really are.

But atoms
    and electrons
Are too small to be seen even by means of the
    microscope.
Only hypothesis tells us they are there.
We can only visualise them as diagrams on a page
Or as models
With coloured wooden balls, and bits of stick holding

them together.
They can't be like *that*.
Then, even knowing only of that unvisualised
                    But existent
                        Thing,
We manage to work around with it
And split it.
'Splitting the atom'.
   All one can visualise is taking a hammer to one of
those models of painted balls and sticks and smashing it.
Sure enough, there's pleasure in the idea.
It would be like smashing an abstraction
– Good riddance!
But no energy can be liberated
From an abstraction.
The energy which holds the atom together
       Is so immense
    That smashing the prototype of the popular diagram
Liberates a force
    So huge
       That it too is in a dimension away beyond us.

Human beings who form concepts in their minds
Are somewhere in between those extremes of vastness
        And infinitesimality,
But human beings
    Are made of atoms, made of electrons held
together by that inconceivably enormous material
force,
        And, human beings,
    We have something else in us even more
inconceivable than that –
        Another force altogether, called 'life'.

'Life' is not a word like 'electron' that puts the
        thing at even greater distance than it is.
'Life' is a word we know about.
    We feel involved with it and
We know what it means,
    Although we can't explain it.
We can explain 'electron'
    Even though we don't really know what it means,

from *origins and elements* (1959)

But 'life' we can't explain.
That's something you just have to accept.

Poetry too
Finally
Is inarticulate
Like Science
Facing wordless wordlessness.

Litmus

I don't know why it is that acid turns blue litmus pink,
And don't tell me you know
Because I'm sure you don't
– 'Because it's acid.' –
That's no reason.
Acid is pink?
Nonsense.
With other reagents the pink's on the other side.
Why pink?
Why blue?
Why change?
And why change only in colour?
I'm not asking to get an answer and an explanation
About the negative logarithm of the concentration of
     free hydrogen ions;
I'm asking for the pleasure of feeling there is no
     answer.
It's magic.

Cave Drawing of the Water of the Earth and Sea

The drops that drop out of the hill
Are destined
To run on to the ocean;
But they'll be back again,
Sure as the salmon
Returns.
One drop is like another drop.
There's always some drop there.
You only feel surprised and discomfited
If a season turns too dry
And no water drips for a time.
But it'll be back all the same.
There are years and years
And if the conformation changes
Something else takes the place of what goes.

Once the drop joins other drops it's no longer a drop,
It's a trickle.
Conjoining trickles stream down the burn,
Hitting the stones and jumping up, for all the world
    gaily,
Making a noise about it,
A sort of chatter
Like distant voices
Or like voices in another dimension.

A whole lot together
Runs deeply and you'd think, slowly,
But it might be swift enough too.
It all depends on the slope of the land.
All the land is in the long run sloping down to the sea.
There might be a hollow
Which the water has to fill up and overflow.
The water then could be a shallow pool
Or a dark dark pool
Or a vast blue lake
And somewhere or other there would be an escape
For it to run out and on down to the sea.

It's a force which draws all movable things towards the
    centre of the earth,

from *origins and elements* (1959)

Which we call, for some reason, gravity.
It seems to exist through and through the whole of
    matter:
So we believe, anyway.
People like to call this sort of thing a 'law'
Because people make *laws*
And want them to be *obeyed*.
So they say that 'obeying the law' of gravity the water
    runs downhill,
Down the merest slope
Until finally the ultimate essential gradient of the
    whole of the land
Causes the river to meet the sea.

The sea too is affected by gravity.
It hugs the circumference of the earth, drawn towards
    the centre.
It doesn't fall off the earth,
Splashing away out into the stratosphere,
Flung as spray off the globe by its daily birling around,
But stays there, swishing about the land.
The moon pulls at it too:
It's not too far way.
The moon's pull is called gravity too,
But it isn't strong enough to pull the water right out
    to it.
What it does is pull and tug at the lumps of water on
    the turning earth
So that first it's going one way
    Then another,
Dashing against the land on one side
Then on the other.
  Isolated bits of land get in the way
And the sea in its mad rush to get to the moon,
  Where, of course, it will never get,
Goes tearing round those islands
    First in one direction
  And then back again.
It never gets anywhere except to where it came
    from,
  But keeps up that reguar surge and heave
    Of the tides

As it hurls itself
for ever towards the moon.

    The kind of drawing the sun does
    Is different.
It uses forces other than gravity.
Its rays of heat
  Insidiously evaporate the surface of the sea
And of the lakes
  And rivers and burns
    And even the wet land the first drop or trickle
      came out of,
All over the world.
Sometimes you see the water rising
  As steam
    Or as a shimmering haze.
It gets drawn well up into the sky
  By the sun.
The time of day and the time of year
Make a difference, of course.
And the place, –
  The sort of place
    And its distance from elsewhere.

Up it goes into the sky, drawn by forces of diffusion,
    convection, and in a way pushed out by earth's
    gravity
Which must have the heavier things nearer always.
But the sun's heat is best felt near sheltering earth.
High up, there's a chill.
Water which was so warm it evaporated (turned to
    gas, water vapour)
Becomes ice.
What exactly happens to it up there is not yet well
    known,
But it collects into bunches
  Of droplets or ice particles
    And makes clouds,
Seen from here as white or grey as the sun's light
    reflects off them,
Or pink, purple, yellow, greenish, or almost any
    colour, in the refracted evening light

from *origins and elements* (1959)

About sunset.
It's all just water
Reflecting light.

One thing or another
  Makes a cloud not be a cloud any more,
And all the water comes down again as rain
  Or as snow
    Or hail or sleet
All just water returning to earth.
The water falling as rain is very pure water
For it was distilled
By that evaporation process.
Dissolved impurities were all left behind.
The salt stayed in the sea, and only the water rose as
      vapour.
As it falls
It picks up and dissolves a little carbon dioxide
From the air.
  If the air is dirty, as it is in cities,
The rain water dissolves some of the dirt too,
Washes it out of the air
But becomes itself dirty water
  Fit to go down the sink.
The rain that falls on cities is city rain.

Within this journey that the water makes
It makes also
  Sub-journeys,
    Detours.
The water gets drunk by us and other animals
And excreted.
It gets sucked up into plants and exuded in the dew,
      which evaporates,
Or is left to evaporate when the plant withers
Or to sink into earth again as it rots.

Some plants and especially the fruits of some plants
      are almost entirely composed of water
With just enough of their own individuality
To transform it completely.

People and all other animals cannot live without water.
It is not life, but it is essential for life,
An element of living in the world.
It's the material we must have to carry life,
        To keep cells from subsiding
    And to bring them substances for their nourishment.
The blood uses water to dissolve essential ingredients
And then push them out into the tissues
By osmosis
It's not possible to explain how it happens,
    But it happens.

This permeation of water into all ourselves
Enables us to keep alive
And to go on thinking of words like 'water'
And to observe phenomena
And presume the existence of others,
    Even explain them
        And make an abstract picture out of magic water.

What is all theory but an abstraction of criss-cross
        Lines,
As the girl proudly said her painting was?
Who the hell cares about criss-cross lines?
An abstraction from a boat scene
    With the boatiness gone
She described as a 'further development from her
        working drawing',
But the drawing had been alive.
The further development was into the grave.

It's all right thinking of the criss-cross lines
If you see them contained in the rest.
But if you think that criss-cross lines are *all* that's
        important,
Well, here's a spade.
Dig yourself a grave.
A spade can be painted
As a thing of lines and planes,
Or it can be painted as a thing to dig graves with.

The rainbow is still a miracle

from *origins and elements* (1959)   53

Even when we know what it's made of,
Or we think we know.
Whether we really know, as perhaps we do,
Or just think we do,
As is very likely,
It's still magic.
It's just there.
Water particles, refracted light, curvature of space,
    might be all part of it
But it's still what it is.
It is still there.
It is irrefutably a miracle.

The water supplied for the life of mankind
Sometimes makes a détour
Into the clouds.
This water I drink from the spring was high in the
    clouds once.
I drink it, so I've been there too.
The dangerous river which drowns men
Was in the sea once.
It's not the first time its water particles have made
    thunder
Or surged darkly.

The water of that diagrammatic circle
Is wet
Because we feel it wet,
And thirst-quenching,
But we'd drown in it.
It belongs a little less to us than to the fishes.

The tide that comes pounding round Orkney
To fill up the North Sea
Is obeying the law of gravity.
– Is that so, now?
The ocean that shatters the rocks
Is having its surface fluffed off into clouds
Which will be ocean again some day.
I drink the ocean
And have met the fish
Which never reach the surface.

Some particle someone gets
Has been in the subterranean passage from the sea into
      Loch Ness,
   If there is one.
Somebody else will get it later,
Or maybe they won't.

Water was made for one purpose only, –
So that I could come to being and write down these
      words here now.
Do you believe that?
I don't,
But it could be argued.

Hooray, Hooray, Hoo Ray Ray Ray

I think the satisfaction
I have got from Science
All my life
Is the realisation
That it's all completely beyond us.
We always feel it's beyond us,
And when we know it too
That's something.
I first heard about radium
When I was ten or eleven,
And it had to be admitted by the teacher
That she didn't really know what she was talking about.
She didn't say so in so many words,
But it showed in spite of her.
Radium
Gives off radiation
And leaves behind lead.
Lead!
But *how?* we all asked.
No 'how' about it. It just does.
What is radiation? 'We don't know.'
Rays.
Rays of what?
And in what?

And there was helium.
It gave off helium too, with the radiation,
And left lead.
But it was an element.
Oh yes, yes, sure, an element.
Look, here it is in the atomic table.
Ra
Radium
And that little symbol there, that's to do with
     radiation.

Is the centre of the sun all lead?
Did all the sun's rays that came here
Make lead and us and the world?
Are all the atoms the same thing really?
Could any one of them give off the thing called
     'radiation'
And helium or some other wispy gas
And leave lead
Or anything else?
Is it all transformable?
And even if it is, does it matter?
That's what the ten-year-olds wondered.

With a hey and a ho and a heigh-ho, heigh-ho,
It could be all anything
But it isn't.
It is what it is.

Mysterious things may be 'given off'
(Given, that's what they say, – *given*)
And leave behind something quite ordinary.
But then it seemed ordinary before, too.
Is what stayed ordinary, or not?
And what went?
Radiation?
'The concentration of radiation in our atmosphere
     has not yet reached danger point.'
A statesman's statement.
He read it off a piece of paper handed to him by an
     atomic physicist,
But what does it mean?

He doesn't know any more than we do.
That's the laugh.

'The effluvium from the atomic power station will be
    discharged into the sea.'
Ever since time began, men have thrown their rubbish
    into the sea,
Thinking in that way they got rid of it.
Royal Navy sailors ashore even throw their rubbish
    out the window
On to the back green
Or front garden
To be washed away by the tide.

It's not easy to get rid of your empty tin cans and
    your waste radiation.
There's something deadly about ragged sardine tins
    under all the house windows
And about clots of radiation in the sea.

Maybe we think we can change all the atoms of the
    world, including ourselves,
Into radiation, helium and lead,
With a few bright photons
For an aurora at the poles
– We can put the poles in a different place too, if we
    want to –
And maybe we're right
But maybe we are thinking through our hats.

Sprung Sonnet

The grief for all the world which grips my heart
Un-nerves me and makes nonsense of the glee
With which I'd greet the Spring.
I would impart,
If there were not the anguish inside of me,
Only my softer thoughts
To word and deed,
Now while the sun shines new and draws the bud.

from *origins and elements* (1959)   57

Laughter gay as daffodils would need
Be unaware
Of blood's cruelty.
Fleecy gaiety
Would have to be too young to know
That new life is conceived in violence,
Born in violence and pain.
The hard green javelins of the flower's birth
Already sharply reject the earth.
There is no time in a creature's life
That comes before the blood-knowledge.
The blood itself knows,
And the first infant yell of unformulated need
Is like the cry from our inner selves
To the walking talking busy ones we are.

Ay, Ay, Ay, Dolores

It's not the time to speak in parables,
But to be outright.
That old Christ there, he told stories
And left it for us to fish out the meaning,
Whenever he felt that the point
Would not be understood otherwise.
Sometimes a fiction
Is more precise and less strange
Than the bleating truth, the facts;
And in a story is perceived
The thing beyond the story.
But sometimes
It is the time to simply to say.
Just say.
But there's so much to say that by the time
  I fine it down there's only one word left
And then that word has to go too, being inadequate,
And only my eyes are left
For saying it all.

Poems, Stories and Writings

from
Subjects and Sequences (1960)

Pomona

Apple blossom and nightingale
Together make a fairy tale
I knew the fairy tale come true.

Night song sweet and sad as Spring.
Filled the garden where the blue
Night hid the apple flower.
Perfume sweeter than the song
Filled the house and garden too.
All night long I heard the song
Till morning illumined the apple tree.

But in the land of the North there are no trees:
In the land of Pomona the apples don't grow.
In the Spring there is no blossom sweet as song
Nor song like honey in the perfumed night.
Instead, we have the flashing white
Seagull cutting the iridescent blue,
The crying blue of sea and sky, the white
Of flying clouds and birds. Oh, who
Would sip the honey in the dark and lose the light?

Sweet honey in the dark sweet song
That stole, continuous and strong,
Every night into the house!
The blossom opened day by day
And, faintly white in the soft night,
Gave perfume to the garden and
The early constant nightingale
Nightly sang the night away.

But in the North the Spring is a hard time;
Bird song pierces and strong winds blow.
Strong birds float softly on the strong sea.
Wild flashing sea stutters on hard green land.
Green cries to us, blue and white laugh at us,
And we stand, buffeted, laughing, crying against the sea.
Oh, who would choose the sweetness and not know
The saltness, flashing whiteness and the strength?

(23 April 1950)
Published in *The Orkney Herald*, 6 May 1958

Bowery

A man was leaning against a tree.
A man was leaning against a lamp-post,
Hyper-extended from head to heels,
Hardly supported, he wavered but did not fall.
His eyes were open but he saw
Only the personages in his dope-dreams.
Eyes open, limbs flaccid, he wore no expression;
No soul no animal looked out from his hanging eyes.
At the angle of the pavement
His air of open depravity went unheeded
By those who slouched in corners eternally waiting
By those who feared and stanched their fears
By those who waited for nothing, hated nothing, loved nothing,
By industrious Chinese walking past.
      They are all lost souls here, the taxi-driver said.
      They are all lost.
Head back against the post, limbs loose, he wavered slightly
               But did not fall.
Where do we go to in our opium dreams?
Where do we come from to this dope-den world?

He must have been a man once; he must once have been a strong man.

Standing Stones of Stenness

The flowers from round the stones
are older than the bones
of vanished worshippers. The rites
here celebrated on nights
of summer solstice by different name,
when the dark that came
so early in other season
waited off, for its own reason
(confirmed and continued, as men knew,
by mystic girations which were then true
but which we have refuted)
are now imputed
to dark ignorance of savage soul

which knew not the golden bowl
and silver cord of witting Word.
Then the bird
was messenger, the seal sharer
of men's secrets, and rarer
secrets of seals in oceans were known by men.
Oh, then
the world was whole, and dark and light
according to man's propitatiations.
Wars between nations
were only preparing in the bitter blight
we made of our earth by our own intellect,
unfailingly unable to be beforehand circumspect.

They are to blame for mistaking
brooks for books
and we, whom they became, for educating
all that is left of them to our worst conclusions.

Fusions
of thought and emotion are to be sought,
– perhaps found (perhaps not).

(1955)
Published in *The Orkney Herald*, 15 April 1958

Then, Oh Then, Oh Then

You are a bird and you chant through my life
Cool as instinct
You are my childhood
Thyme tincture and coppersmith
Lustless
Red flowers on the bare
Pale white trees where the egrets were
Tree that before the leaves came had
Large red flowers
Cottonwood
No! Silk-cotton tree
For when the fruit fell after the leaves formed

Flaming flowers had ripened soft seed-down
Secure and essential
Useful for the honey-sucker's nest.

The tree the flowers the song
Were there before continue now
I absent.

Coincidences punctuate
Slur and stress our separate activities.

(1952)
(To T.D. ApI)

Edward Nairn, Poet

A heightened, fevered and yet deliberate way,
A fine line along the ridge,
A high-held muzzle in the rushing wind.

Out of the trees, in the forest of heather and green,
Terrain of deer and pheasant, open forest, sky-bound,
Edward goes sedately and yet flies,
For though soles tread earth he snuffs high the cloud-air,
The blue and the grey air filled full of curlews' calls.
This high oxygen feeds the topmost brain-cells
(Ozone for neurons of irreplaceable one-ness)
And they respond with their one-only kind of song and truthfulness,
Merely produce it,
Enter it there and draw a neat line.

(5 June 1955)

from *Subjects and Sequences* (1960)   63

Kulgin the Helicopter

Hovering
With pre-determined vagueness,
He makes as if to land but then forbears,
Decides
Not to stop there, decides to flit again.
Fuelled in passing, fuelled in air perhaps,
Accepting contributions from the temporary pump,
The helicopter leaps, settles like a flea and leaps again.
Decision there is, all in a different phase from ours.

Unrelated to the sap-sucking flower span,
The bee darts and pauses and later returns to its own organised hive.
But where is the helicopter honeycomb?
What is its ultimate plan?
Is there some spoon-fed silk-clad helicopter queen waiting to be
    nourished from the short flights' products?
Ask the helicopter.
No more the bee knows its destined objective
As it frantically flits, makes an end and flits again.

(5 June 1955)

Alex

I think nothing of your thought-out thought,
But value you thinking it.
The you-ness of you is other than that.
The troubled deep runner
And angry expostulator differ.

Tingling stream
contains the pounding sea-beat surge
(But not to explain it,
Not to expound it).

Starlings wheel
And know which moment to.

In the long journey homeward
The lemmings drown,
But down the road you take
Head-above-water you go.

Over and over again
The weaver fashions
Over and over
Warm germ-plasm beds down;
And over
Shrieks a thought
Above the ice of you of the you of the you.

(1957)

Allison

My friend is dead, my sweet sweet sister is gone,
But her coat still hangs on the wall
And her younger son runs along the lobby
To look round the bedroom door.
'Away,' he remarks, in baby disappointment, 'away, away, away!'

Dear girl who became my sister,
Could she be not dead, but sleeping?
Will she awake with the flowers on her grave
And tell us once again her happy song?
Allison, I fear not.

She died.
It was a positive act and has no undoing.
There is no undoing of death. It is an end.
But all ends are ends. Is this then more of an end
More an end than the end of a day,
More than the end of a year
Or of an old life, a lived-out life?
All she did is as alive as all we did.
In her house I feel her presences.
Essential child girl and woman affect us and will do so.
In her little son who cannot remember her I see her,

from *Subjects and Sequences* (1960)   65

And in the bigger boy who remembers her well I see her too
And hear her.
Unbroken survival of the germ makes of brief being a heritage.
Perhaps in three, five, twenty generations
Shall live another Allison.
I shall not know, nor my descendants, for I have none.
But Allison continues
Not only in what she has sung,
Not only in what she has written, or done,
Not only in what she has said to us or told to the children,
But in those children's selves,
Their genes and chromosomes,
Their cells and nuclei, fears and reflexes,
Their laughter and their tears,
And even the inflexion of the voice.

She liked roses and the scent of southernwood.
She liked the daffodils in the park.
She liked to laugh, and singing, she said, was a physical pleasure.
She liked the poets of mediaeval Scotland
And the high tenements of a city
But dearly she lived and died in the lovable North.
Orkney was to Allison like an enchantment
Which she accepted and entered when she accepted my brother.
Inside the magic circle she lived
And died.
I can only lament.
I can only weep and wish she were alive;
And I re-examine,
Was there something to notice that we didn't notice?
Could some positive perception have possibly saved her?

Until her last breath she must have been happy:
She was always happy.
Until her last heart-beat her feelings were gay:
She had such a dancing spirit.
Until the moment she left she felt secure,
So confident was she.

And so she laughed her life away,
As she dismissed all weary cares,
And so she sang and so she told us

Happy hopeful genial airs.
Until the day the blood came pouring,
Tore placenta from the wall,
And Death leapt out from his lair in the dark,
Bytuene Mershe and Averil,
And lyht on Alysoun.

But why not try this method

Empty it out and put in what they said.
Sshh! Don't mention the truth.
Fill it all full of tricks and gewgaws,
Then you'll win.
Twist the barrel of the rifle and hit that sly bullseye on the side.
There's one to suit you.
That is, if you're sly too, there is.
Don't attempt it with poetry;
Nobody wants your true words.
Don't dare offer love,
For that is obscene.
Prink it up and follow the feature pages,
Work it all out and lay the trap,
Set it in all the falseness you can think of,
And, that way, you own darling of your own self,
You can't fail.
Never in a million can you fail that way.

(October 1957)

A Poem for a Morning

I'm out here now
on the roof. Look!
I had to get nearer the sky,
For the city was too full of rooms
And I can't be content with a window.

It's too small a thing to accept the ready-made frame.
We builders must keep making our own cities.
Oh, please
Don't fell the trees
For your city, because I need them for mine.

(1958)

Pavement Artist

I chalk it out on the ready squares.
Only the colours out of the box
Are available.
If you walk
And scrape your shoe on the finer lines
I do them over, with emphasis.
But a sort of blur
Is the result of too much walking
And, in the blur,
Exaggeration and some distortion,
Result of making too often the journey.

Told to die,
I can't die without dying.
How can I?
For my ninety lives are at an end.
I've inhabited too many Margarets
And there aren't any more left.

Restless spirits go a-haunting,
So they used to say.
Mine will have sport for centuries
If that's the way:
Spilling of the ink-pot,
Tearing of the page,
Intruding with blundering fingers
In the micro-picture gauge.

What would you think
If I took to shouting?

What would you think
If I skipped the length of the street?
Or slapped the faces of strangers?
Or cheeked the policeman on the beat?
What would you say if I burst out crying
And cried that I couldn't manage alone?
What would you do if I gave up trying
And sat on a stone
And never came home?

Who are these crowds in me
If I am myself alone?
What are these other voices I hear
And what are the hands that tug me here and there?
I am all of my ancestors,
Seafarers and landsmen,
Ale-tipplers and cake-bakers,
And ravagers of homes and fields.
All the troubled women
And all the striding ship-men,
Labouring land-workers,
Up-striving sad merchants,
Mourning mothers, dotty grandmas
And well-wishers, ill-wishers,
Doers and undoers
Lodge here in my high heath
Where I light my fire.

I lit the light-house for you
To guide you in the mirk.
You'll see the regular flashing,
You'll count,
And by the known timing,
By recognition of that formula once learned
You'll know it's me.

It's in myself, this mazy thing,
This unattachable me,
This floating footless creature,
This last word in what shouldn't be.

(21 October 1957)

from *Short Poems on Blue Paper*

Children are prose,
But poetry's their world.
With those early eyes
They see
What we don't see,
But will be
What we are.

Someone in Scotland made a picture
Which was so full of feeling
That they had to destroy it at once.
It was too too too
Just too too.
Well ——!
They've now made a law
So that nothing like that can ever happen again.
After all, they mean to say, well,
Decency must be preserved.

Historical Sense

Fifty-seven, fifty-eight, fifty-nine, sixty, sixty-one, sixty-two, –
I was counting.
Nine million and twelve, nine million and thirteen, nine million
    and fourteen.
Well, well, time passes.
A billion billion million and three.
Soon all the time will be taken just in the counting.
Soon only the residue of counted steps will be left.

Can the words ever reach where the love can't?
Sometimes a message out of the past
Seems to heal for a little.
An indication
That another suffered
The same bitter annihilation
Saves for a little while
A similar soul from extinction.

Water
Washes guilt away,
So the Christians say;
But all the tears that I can weep
Can't wipe clear
The smear
That Christian teaching made
On my self-knowing sorrowing soul.

(October 1957)

The Old Lady of Loth

The fire to burn me made
A bonny sicht
And, here! I held oot me hauns
To the leapin licht,
For I never thocht but what
It wis to waarm me.
I wis thinkan o me hoosie
Wi' bare a turf
To heat the poor lassie
Wha's all me care.
I thocht it wid be fine
To ha'e sic a like lowe there.
Mercy! The folk must ha'e wunnered
To see me smilan bonny
Afore the stink o' me body
Burnan in the sweet air
Sent them home coughan and chokan.

Published in *The Orkney Herald*, 10 December 1957

from *Subjects and Sequences* (1960)

Punishment

Was it Calvin who told you that you are God?
Old John Knox who muttered, 'Don't trust the women'?
And the two of them together
Sniggering and lording it there in their black garments

No doubt it was they
Whispered and secretly urged you while you were still a little
      embryo in the womb
That you would be
Ultimately and utterly
Responsible
For your own actions and also for what happens to others.

Love is more costly than comfort.
It's worth more, of course,
And it certainly costs more to get it
Or even to give it;
For we pay out our entrails for it and with it,
Whereas comfort is bought with simple labour alternating
      with indolence.

Most people do contract out
And settle for the smaller thing.
That's why there are so few poets, of course.

Poets are more responsible than other people, because of
      understanding more,
So poets cannot escape punishment.

One World, One Sun

The sun in Jhansi was a sort of enemy.
All the dwellings were built against it,
Not to entrap it
As we try here.
I can remember that beating feeling on my head.
In Johore, I saw a yellow circle slipping down into the sea at the
      very same time each day
– Round about six –

And golden orioles came into the trees too, daily
About that time of day.
I remember being conscious that I would miss the constancy of the
    light
More than the heat.
In Orkney the north light is magic and inconstant,
Illuminating in a poignant way
I never saw in the East,
Because in the East I was further south.
In the high Himalayas there was a light which reminded me of home,
Of the sea.
Mountains remind me of the sea
And mountain people remind me of island people.
One day in Surrey when I was observing the early morning light
    minute by minute
While the escholtzia opened,
I felt I was in Kashmir.
As I followed the gradual opening of the flower petals
Some quality of the light transported me there to the gardens of
    petals in the high mountains
Where schoolchildren brewed tea in a samovar,
Shrilling in their own language and wearing round caps with a
    pointed crown.
I seemed to see the very colour of the sun the same,
Perhaps because I was watching the petals.
The sun in Jhansi reflected off the ground and hit us in the face
    under the brims of our hats,
Hit us with heat and with light too,
Both the light and the heat tiring the human frame,
Disintegrating the well-put-together human instrument;
And we took refuge in dark rooms with a fan turning
And sprinkled lukewarm water to cool us by evaporation.
In Britain we cheer up at sight of the sun and run outside so as
    not to miss it.
The sun is our friend here, we are sun-seekers,
Not sun-shunners like the dwellers of sunnier lands.
We burst into smiles as the sun bursts out and sadden when the
    clouds cover it.
We go around singing because of a cloudless sky.

In Jhansi, we watched the bare sky, day after day hoping for a
    man's-hand cloud of rain.
We waited, panting, for the downpour.

from *Subjects and Sequences* (1960)   73

We wished the sun away,
Feared it
And took all precautions against it.

On days by the sea in Scotland the sun can be more than is good
      for you.
Its excessive ultraviolet can seriously debilitate.
Temporarily
It can exhaust and sicken the human body.
Too much brilliance and too much penetration by the high frequency
Jangles,
Does something to the equilibrium of vital centres.
In that kind of brilliance with a dazzling haze the blue is beyond
      the blue.
The eyes are stunned by too enveloping light
And by too blueness.
A slanting light of September picks out individual grasses.
An early morning light in summer makes dew-covered foliage
      sparkle.
A late sun warms the red flowers and colours the houses.
Windows seem to have red lamps set in them
And white surfaces turn rosy.
All over the sky the fire edges out to turquoise, to lemon and
      stupendous purple,
Variegating for hours in a northern night
When the sun sets almost at midnight
And the dawn glow shows before the last colours fade.

I saw the round ball rise in the winter out of the sea,
Shooting out rays in straight quivering lines
With even some colour change
Like an aurora
Borealis.
Aurora (dawn) it was anyway.

I watched the midwinter sun go down early in almost the south.
Its weak light all day had been scarcely actinic,
And to look straight at it then, low towards the south,
Caused no trouble to the eye nor to the photographic layer.
I bathed with delight in the sun as I sat on the warm stones
In worn but not care-worn Italy.
The sun is kind to Italy.
It loves Italy and Italy loves the sun.

They sing, 'O sole mio,' – O my sun, they sing.
They feel the sun is for them, and so it is, maybe.
In Italy the sun is very kind, both in its kind of light and its kind
    of heat,
Not brutal
Like a tropical or equatorial sun,
Nor whimsical, variable, poignant like the sun of the north,
But just there,
Warming, lighting
People and their lives,
And lighting the gracious man-made miracles in stone or paint or
    marble or wood,
Lighting up the colours chosen
And lighting the natural colour and texture of the material.
Italy's light is a light for man-made wonders.
It is kind.
It is a tender, realistic light.
The piercing light of the north sometimes shows up man-made
    things as shoddy.
It makes us ashamed
There in its brilliance.
In the kind Mediterranean smiling illumination
No one feels ashamed,
Not really ashamed
Of simply doing whatever they have to do.

The brilliant piercing light of the north of the world
Makes us feel at the mountain tops,
Makes us feel high up in the luminous sky,
But makes us feel, sometimes, inadequate to be there.
Miraculous excessive light of the north of it all
Shows man himself,
Brilliantly shows the man and the woman themselves,
Ecstatically pushes at hills,
Seizes flowers, thrusting them at us vividly,
And seems to lift the sea and spatter on clouds and point vehemently
    at all moving objects.
It needs great courage to live in the north light.
We would need to have the courage of children, to live here
    undismayed.

(1958)

Epiphany

Out of the deep dark sleep of winter
I return to the light.
The white
Sun
Is here again.
The deep stirrings
In engendering night
Swerve,
Enlarge,
Take wider circles, and cast shadows now,
Throw their images before them or behind.
I'm out now,
Out of the leaf-bed,
Spurting and sprouting up from the humus
And into the day.

(6 January 1958)

Northerner

It's the now of all the now
– Now intensified –
For the solstice has been
When the days stood still:
The darkest time of all
– Dark of a darkness made for renewal –
    that I crawled into
    and lay in,
(Dark, dark the winter keeping)
Waiting, oh waiting for the sun.
In its absence, though,
Knowing of sun there, of
Sun's own healing, growing, drawing qualities,
Nursing the deep power of the sun.

Poems, Stories and Writings

My north is turning to the sun
And will have long light days,
Will have the light I need
But from which I must recover later
By next long winter of dark days,
Short, dark, inside, budding, moiling,
    hibernating days and long nights.

(January 1958)

Midwinter

Where the sun sets in midwinter
It shines up the south-pointing passage of Maeshowe
And enters warmly at ground level the big stone chamber so deeply
    dark for the rest of the year.

The single standing stone in the field there is a little to the west.
West again is the group of huge standing stones,
And the sentinel,
And the Ring of Brogdar, great stone circle.

No wonder the early inhabitants of the young islands
Raised monoliths.

I would have set up stones too
For such an event
As the sun going down behind the hills of Hoy
And then, while it's away, turning
So that next day it sets a little further west,
And day after day a little further west and a little further north,
Until in the long midsummer days
Which have only twilight instead of dark
The sun going down almost in the north
Merely dips and rises –
But turns again,
Rises always a little further east and south,
Sets a little more west and south.

from *Subjects and Sequences* (1960)   77

Oh, anyone at all would have made a circle,
Trailed new-cut heavy stones from anywhere
– From far away –
Monstrous stones needing many men to lug them,
And have raised then upright, pointing to the sky
To stand with shadows sloping
And signify
The mystery of the sun's progress.

(8 January 1958)
Published in *The Orkney Herald*, 18 March 1958

You Heard What the Minister Said, Pet

Hell fire and damnation
Are for the sin of the flesh.
The sin of the flesh we can't explain:
You won't understand it yet, dear.

Adam was the first man, the first man, the first man,
Adam was the first man and Eve the wicked lady.
Come and get your wedding gown wedding gown wedding gown,
Come and get your wedding gown, my fair lady.
Out the garden you must go you must go you must go
Out the garden you must go, –

'Death, disaster and destruction
Are too good for the likes of her
All the sins of the world are female;
The Fall of Man is simply Woman.'

Why does the minister scream, ma,
And what is he saying?
Ma, I'm frightened when he bellows like that.

Don't speak so loud, look, here's a sweetie.
You're too young to understand.
He's speaking against the lust of the flesh.
He wants all girls and boys to be good.

I'm a little gurl and I have a little curl
Right in the middle of my forehead.
When I am good I'll be very very good,
And when I am bad I'll be a
Grownup lady
  With lipstick
    And babies,
      Twins in a pram
And a great big washing machine.

'The eyebright was for you'

The eyebright was for you
And the corn marigolds
– I had a pailful of them –
And the pallid seed-boxes of black seeds there in the coffee-cup
– They're still there –
And a thistle that was splendid when I cut it;
Heather, asphodel, berries, moss,
Gentian
I carried for you.
Those things wither, but there's always next year.
Then, on the last day of delay
– the day I took the marigolds from among the oats –
I gathered stones for you,
Smoothed, yellow, glistening grey, some almost pink, some blue,
And the stones you still could feel, if you will,
Weigh in your hand,
Stroke the surface of,
And sense from weight, surface, size, the inherent shape of them,
Know from their outward qualities
What they are made of and what forces formed them.

Bushels

Women under bushels,
Extinguished lights,
Women poets
– Poetesses –
You never had a chance, had you?

They either dressed you in blue stockings
Or put you in the kitchen.
You could be gracious
    or gossipy
    or good cooks,
'Motherly,'
Or, if not that, then 'manly,' they insisted,
Never strong, feminine, yourselves,
Not that, never that,
Never women, poetesses,
Beings and doers in your own right.

Mary, Queen of Scots

Mary came dancing.
Oh, what a crime!
Mary was entrancing, –
A sin in the eyes of the Lord.
The black-coated gentlemen
Knew fine the Lord's wishes in the matter.
Well they knew
That ladies are not for decoration nor for pleasure
And certainly not for any activity of the mind
Other than serving
Their lords and masters,
Men
Made in the image of God.

Women were not made in the image of anything,
Because of course there is no Goddess for them to made in the
    image of,
Only a God

With a voice like thunder
– Or soft-spoken when he appears on earth in the form of his own
    Son –
And a long white beard
Or a wispy black one, according to which is more suitable in the
    circumstances.

So Mary was supposed to squash herself
Into the man-made corsets
Of staid deportment,
Seemly deference to her statesmen
And ear-drum-shattering demands that she change her church
    IMMEDIATELY.
Mary was young.
She imagined life was for enjoying.
She imagined that sensible people would listen to her.
But she was wrong.

I wonder what she did to pass the time, all those years in prison.
She must have been relieved, in the end, to get her head cut off.

Published in *The Voice of Scotland*, vol. 9, no. 1, 1958

Secrets

Why does Lawrence want us to be secret?
Why does he say that women's secret mustn't be told?
It isn't a secret really, it's only a mock secret
Kept secret on purpose for some purpose of man's,
Kept secret to keep women under covers,
Hidden so that men can hide women away for themselves,
Each what he can get for himself,
Like a dog burying a bone.
The dog thinks the bone should be kept secret
And not exposed to the world,
For then it is destroyed.

The idea of secret is all tied up with the idea of sin.
Man invented the idea that woman is sin
And forced her to be secret

Like a secret sin.
All covered up and hidden and stowed away
Like a sin.

And the male missionaries go to the African tribes and tell them to
    cover up and consider themselves sinful.
They hand them hideous calico garments sewn reluctantly by
    unhappy schoolgirls
And say to put them on and hide themselves.
The lady missionaries tell them the same thing,
For they have been covered up and made secret long ago
And everyone thinks their own way is the right way.

What beats me is that the naked happy women listen to them.
I suspect it isn't they who listen at all
But their men
Who suddenly are given the intoxicating idea of making their
    women secret
And by God will do so.
The Bible says batter the women,
Hide the bones of your women in a corner of the garden,
'Your' women,
Keep them secret, all happed up in the idea of sin,
Then you'll be safe, old man.

Ah yes, Mr Lawrence, you are wrong.
I have to tell you you are wrong,
And I can say so
Because you are wrong
– Not about the pomegranates, though,
About the figs, –
Wrong about women and their secret,
Because the time of women is at hand
And the good will come of the secret not being secret any more.

from

The Hen and the Bees (1960)

Hen

Hen
Means honey, means hinny,
Means endearment,
Means comic assessment,
– Only slightly comic, –
means dear,
means it's a little funny isn't it that we have this
  attachment to each other,
Means we're all alike,
Means peck, peck, peck,
Means a word is a word,
Means dearie,
Means you and me both,
Means you, stranger, are something to me,
Means you, my wee thing, are ma ain wee thing,
Means hinny,
Means honey.

Dogs

I hate dogs.
Disgusting caricatures of human and animal life,
Neither one thing nor the other,
Pets
Made to function for human diversion –
To divert people.
That's all they're good for, those pets.
Working dogs are all right.
They have a life of their own, intact, self-limiting,
With some dignity,
But those undignified fawners, jumpers-up, liers-
  before-the-fire,
Vomiters and swallowers of their own vomit,
Pet dogs,
Lap dogs –
I certainly wouldn't want them on *my* lap.
No wonder they give people asthma!

Family

Pertelot summoned Chanticleer
To come in under and shelter with the chicks.
But Chanticleer was wiser
And knew not to do that
And be smothered with a kind of attention meant only
    for infants.
So he stayed out and free,
Crowing his head off,
And she found truly the house was more itself
With only the cheeping hungry chicks under her wing,
Running out and in as chicks do,
And Chanticleer out there being Chanticleer
Not pretending to be a chick too.

The Scale of Things

There's a whole country at the foot of the stone
If you care to look
These are the stones we have instead of trees
In the north.
Our trees all got lost,
Blown over or cut down
Long long ago, and some of them lie there still in the
    peat moss
Or fossilised in limestone.
At the shady foot of trees
Certain things grow,
But at the foot of stone grow the sun-loving
    wind-resisting short plants
With very small bright flowers
And compact, precise leaves.
The wind whips the tight stems into a vibration,
But they don't break.
The full light of the sun reaches right down to the
    ground,
And reflects obliquely and sideways in among and
    under the snug leaves,
And settles on the stone too,

from *The Hen and the Bees* (1960)

Makes a glow there,
A sufficient warmth and clarified light.
The stunning frequencies seem to get absorbed
And if you stare closely at the stone
It's a calm light, not too blue,
Precisely indicating its variegated surface.
The great stone stands,
On a different scale, in a way, from the minute plants
     at its base.
A proliferating green lichen
Grows on it
As well as round golden coin-patches of another
     common lichen,
And only in the earth right up to the very stone but
     not on it
Grow the crisp grass
And all the tiny plants and flowers
Which, together interlaced and inter-related,
Make the fine springing turf which people and animals
     walk on.

*

At the bottom of the window box
There are stones.
You can't see them.
They came from a small river called the Heriot
     Water,
And some were greenish
From something growing on them.
Slime, it is called –
A growth, a vegetable.
I put the earth on top of them
And now you can't see the stones.
The roots of the plants growing there go down
     towards them.
Perhaps some good comes off them, or perhaps they
     are simply drainage.

Published in *The Orkney Herald*, 23 September 1958

Poems, Stories and Writings

Locklessness

No locks.
No bolts, bars nor keys.
It's all wide open.
Wearing the blinkers
Keeps the horse going straight:
It sees no distraction.
That way, with blinkers on, it's a society mare.
I hate harness.
I see it's cosy for others.
I see people need it
Or want it,
But *I* don't want it
– Not for keeps.
I can use it or not use it
According to the needs of the eventuality.

Throw away the keys!
Smash the locks!
Leave the door wide open for thieves to enter!
Let them take it –
They can have it.
Let them take the lot, for I can do without.
Where the things go makes very little difference.

For Using

Material things are only tools
Or they're nothing.
Food is a sort of tool,
Fire is a warming tool,
And paint-brushes, pencils, cameras, books
All tools of a kind
For making a life
Or lives.
But too much food is poison,
Comfort a permanent anaesthetic,
And too many paint-brushes, cameras, books
Waste away as toys.

from *The Hen and the Bees* (1960)

A tool has the feel of the user's hand on it
If it's a real tool.
A tool that is fully used
Gets a bloom on it
From its own essential-ness.
All other bits and things are clutter.

(March/April 1958)

Light

Did you say it's made of waves?
Yes, that's it.
I wonder what the waves are made of.
Oh, waves are made of waves.
Waves are what they are,
Shimmeringness,
Oscillation,
Rhythmical movement which is the inherent essence
    of all things.
Ultimately, there's only movement,
Nothing else.
The movement that light is
Comes out of the sun
And it's so gorgeous a thing
That nothing else is ever anything unless lit by it.

(March/April 1958)

Responsiveness

It's possible to walk
And step only on the bits of a certain pattern,
But then you can't help wondering how it feels
To go on the other bits only.
Children make those explorations.
They have to,
But the more inquisitive ones soon learn to walk on

it all equally,
Feeling with the sole of the foot,
Even through the shoe-sole,
Minute differences of configuration and surface
As well as biggish boulders
And crevices, cracks, loose rubble, sand, growing
    grass, beaten mud.
The feet transmit the knowledge of those things
Up through the limbs
Not only by messages about surface sensations
But also by actual transmission
Of the jarring of hard stone
Or the give of sand, calling for tension to resist it.
Slipperiness,
Resilience,
Bog
All find their way upwards in the give or the spring
    we use to respond to them.

Trust

I like you to extend out in all your endless
    possibilities.
I like you to inhabit the multitudes you contain.
I like to know that a lot of your being is away beyond
    me
As a lot of me is beyond you.
The trust relates to that part,
To the unknown.
I trust you to know or feel what to do with your own
    unknown,
And I trust you to trust me to be in the me unknown
    to you honest and not in the end forgetful of you.

from *The Hen and the Bees* (1960)

Spring 1958

The buds this year
Are stuck and can't get out
Into leaf.
All the northern world is deep frozen.
The flowers refuse to enter
The air which is solid and grey.
The lambs are dismayed
At the cheerless earth they have been dropped on to
And stand there, shocked and hardly even shivering,
It's such a disappointment.
After a mere blink
Of sunshine
The frost returns
And the obliterating snow
Wetly covers the sprouting breir.

The birds
Keep very quiet,
And children stay indoors.

(April 1958)

Remains that Have Been Tampered With

The stone shouldn't be like that.
The altar is an artifact
And should be dismantled.
There it stands,
Suggesting human sacrifice
To our suggestible minds,
But there wasn't sacrifice
And there shouldn't be sacrifice.
It's all artifact,
Intellectual,
Intended, and false.
There wasn't really sacrifice on the stone.
Someone coming after wanted to make it look like
        that.

Someone coming recently,
Long after the time,
Made a false altar
And pretended it came down from the original.
The stone was not a table
For spilling blood on.
It was upright.
It should be set upright again
Or at least tossed off to lie in the grass, a fallen stone
    and not an invented would-be place of sacrifice.

Published in *The Orkney Herald*, 1958

Queen of Fact and Story

In the perpendicular window,
Her robe hung out from her shoulders
Flying on a current of air surrounding her –
A breeze which gently lifted the purple silk apart from
    her naked body.
So the veined skin,
The lucent nipples,
The shadowy umbilical depression
And the tight curled hair
On the mount of Venus
All shone
In a veiled soft purple-blue-ness
Of sunlight
Filtering through silk.
Beyond, through the window,
The apples glittered on the tree.
Boughs of red fruit
Twisted out to the sky and hung to the sun
To ripen.
At the tree's root
A fresh green shoot grew.

Near the queen, on the floor,
Lay the lioness.
The lion eyes glowed

Like bowls of copper
Inverted,
Curiously metallic and unpopulated.
The beast lay coiled like a spring,
Purring with warmth,
Awaiting some attention from the queen.

The queen herself had eyes
Full of legends.
She left her body naked
As a decoration for the room,
And through her eyes told stories
For the delectation
Of men
And women
And children
Who came to see her.

(April 1958)

Story-telling Queen

They were all a little dazed
At the stories she told.
They came out of her ancestral memory,
And, as her ancestors were their ancestors,
They recognised the characters.

When she began a story
They gathered round
And settled into comfortable positions
Within reach of the fire.
From the first few sentences
They knew the tone of it
And adjusted their consciousness accordingly.
The modulations of her voice
Made the words sound like music.
Details of events
Reverberated like song.
Precisely recounted happenings

Chimed
And a refrain of the usual outcome went singing away
    off into nowhere.

The children's eyes stared,
Sleepy though the children were,
For they felt themselves taken bodily into the story.
The older people, being more sceptical,
Rolled the tale over like epicures
Relishing a titbit
And added it to the slow accumulation
Of lore in their flesh.

The queen told all she could
Until the tale ended,
And her tale went into their store
While in her own store she sought about for the next
    legend for them.

(April 1958)

Sea-going King's Queen

He was a king of the sea-going kind,
With the sky in his eyes.
During his long expeditions
She ruled the land
And told tales to the children
Of the far-going longships out on the ocean.
She told the long story
Of older fighting kings then dead
Whom they all knew by name.

She picked the shells off the seashore
And the children set them on sandy flat stones in the
    wind
And made up games.
Sometimes they learned the names
– Pet names for common shells, mostly –
And the names entered the games.

from *The Hen and the Bees* (1960)   93

The children's fingers were clumsy for placing the
        shells on the stones
But fine for picking them up
And for the careful sifting among the soft sand
Such as the queen showed them
As the way to find the delicate pink fans and other
        shapes,
Subtly coloured and intricately marked,
Which they then set out in order on a stone
To gaze at
And to arrange and re-arrange.

In some big shells they heard the sea,
And nearby, too, the sea itself
Roared
Or sandily swished,
So they weren't likely to forget the king afar in his
        ship fighting.

(April 1958)

The Queen and All the Children

The children of the palace were not all the queen's
        children,
For some were children of her serving maids.
Her own sons and daughters were all king's children,
And of the others some were and some weren't.

The queen offered suck
To other infants.
Her nipple was well-known
To many tiny mouths fitting over it at different times.
Their later love for her acknowledged that she cast
        them off early to be themselves,
To play at mud palaces
And fall in the burn
And then to climb high and be bruised and recover
And gradually expand and grow in their own way.
All that time they were fed and cared for by the
        serving women,

Their mothers, whom they loved,
But they remembered too, in their memory before
    memory,
The queen's milk which helped to form early
    bones.

The queen told stories
To her children and the other children
Equally.
She spoke out to them all,
And she showed them
Where the particular plants grew
That came up year by year
Each in its own place.
She taught them to listen
For individual messages
From water against a stone
Or from birds flying high
Or from unseen things scraping under earth.
From the very words she used
They learned
How to be the children of that place
And how to be and feel like the people of that place
    only.
They grew
In their own way,
Which was the way for the people who lived among
    those sounds and among those stones and hills and
    grasses
And with the scent of the wind in that place only
    reaching them.

A Queen in Prison

When the queen's child was born, they took the baby
    right away from her.
She never even knew whether it was a son or a daughter.
They never told her.
They gave her pills to stop her breasts lactating:
'To stop the milk and ease the pain,' they said,

And she, counting yet once more against her will
The number of bars across her window,
Swallowed.
'She's taking it well, ' they said,
And they felt relieved,
Smiling to each other in the passages and far rooms
     of the prison.
For she might have made a scene,
And then where would they have been?
They didn't quite notice when she began to go mad,
For it was a slow process,
But it gradually and inevitably happened.
She never tore at the bars,
But sat and counted them, hour after hour, aloud,
Each time ending on a short laugh
Which got on the nerves of her attendants.

For years she lived like that,
With frequent changes of attendant,
For no one of them could stand it for very long.

                              *

The king has ta'en his eldest son
     And led him in the fray
He thocht to teach him the battle sense
     Afore he gaed away.

The king gaed up and he gaed up
     Against the enemy
His young son followed him behind
     Learning to fight the fray.

They hadna gaen a pace, a pace
     A pace but barely three
Afore they found them face to face
     Wi the weirdsome enemy.

The king he focht and sairly focht
     To drive them all away
And when they'd gaen and he thocht o his son
     The lad was near away.

'Oh father, father,' his young son said,
    'Father, it hurts me sair.
I thocht to dae sae muckle wi me life
    And noo I'll dae it nae mair.'

The king cam hame wi his son in his arms
    The queen cried 'Lackaday!
Whatever made you think sae early to teach him
    The workings of the fray?'

(20 April 1958)

Belief

'There isn't such a thing as a queen.'
They all said,
'Only kings' wives,
Women
Like other women,
Just honoured, that's all, by being selected, wanted.
Women have to be wanted, or they're no good.
So what are called queens are merely the women the
    kings have selected;
because, unfortunately, men can't do without women.
If they could,' they said,
'Things would be better.
Handiest way of getting a housekeeper, though,
– Marry a woman.
Then you needn't pay her and you won't lose her.
She knows which side bread's buttered.
But – queens!
Well!
What an idea!
As if there could be queens, we mean natural queens,
Women with possibilities of their own.
Don't make us laugh,' they said,
And laughed, just the same.

from *The Hen and the Bees* (1960)

Other Gods, Other Ways

I don't believe anyone worshipped those gods.
The relationship was quite different.
They were superior friends, rather,
And not always even so superior.
They were fallible
As the invention of the Jews is not fallible.
Christ, I think, tried to soften that terrible Jehovah
    concept
While keeping its validity.
But he couldn't do both,
And we've now the choice of the bog of self-sacrifice
Or the bare Moses-rock precipice of self-righteousness.
But long ago the gods here
Came and went
Among the stones,
Intent about their own business
And without the ferocious responsibility
Which the missionaries taught us.
Columba,
Augustine,
And the Knox
And finally the high priests of the Disruption,
Preaching
A natural aristocracy
But teaching, in spite of themselves,
Mean equality,
Got us all in such a muddle that we no longer know
    who we are.

The gods then
Walked about
On equal terms.
The gods then
Had their own affairs to see to.
The old gods of northern people
Didn't ask for bull's blood
And they didn't expect
Bowing down nor self-extermination
By any of us.
Suicide was unknown of, then.

The gods then
Had a similar relationship with people
To what people had with animals
– Had *then*,
For now we don't know how to meet the animals
     either.

It was Christ who spoilt it all,
Quite against what he thought he was doing.
He meant well
But oh, he didn't know about the natural northern
     gods
Coming and going
Among the people,

Casually regarding the building of the stone circles
Which had something to do with them
But something to do too
With something away beyond them again.

Published in *The Voice of Scotland*, vol. 9, no. 1, 1958

Loki Beside the Standing Stone

One of the gods, called Loki,
Not very popular with the others,
Sat against the stone, and pondered.
The stone was one of a circle
Raised
By men in honour of something they didn't understand.
Loki neither
Understood,
But he liked the feeling of the great stone behind him,
Rough with jagged crumbly lichen
And warm, in a way, from the sun,
Yet inwardly cold, cold as stone keeps inwardly cold
     in the north;
And as he sat there, pressing his back against the flat
     stone,
Some comfort came from it

And he felt less hopeless
About his own tiresome tendency
To play pranks which somehow always ended in
    disaster.
He realised
That if that was really his inherent character
He had to keep on like that
And never mind if nobody liked him.

(April 1958)

Thor

Thor was less of an animal god –
More abstract than the others.
He was the thunder itself,
The mineral power,
Electricity in the air.
We'd say now he was controlled by sunspots
And more active every eleven years.
And we'd say, too,
'No, it's not the atomic explosions affecting the
    weather,
It's Thor.'
His resounding, rumbling name suits him.
He rumbles round the earth, reverberating off it,
But he remains controlled from elsewhere.
He is more powerful than human beings trying out
    nuclear missiles in the desert
But he is not more powerful
Than the repetitive phenomena of the sun
Which must have some further and further and further
    control beyond.

Freya

There's a cloudy grey and white woman among them,
Matronly
And rather scolding.
That's my impression of her.
A strong woman, tremendously sad,
Who rides across the clouds, ordering things,
Loving too strongly,
Loved too but feared by the men-gods.
They had the sort of fear of her
That made them giggle and run off.
She was the mother-figure, scolding them
And
She was youth and agelessness
And age
And comfort, wholeness, steady shelter.
But she kept driving across the clouds,
Searching.

Baldar

Odin as head of the family
Of gods,
Was tolerant and wise-like.
He ordered the feast, though,
With thirteen at the table,
And Baldar the beautiful, young and last to come
Had to be sacrificed.
The pattern came again in another story
When thirteen at table
One was crucified.
There wasn't an Odin among the company at table
    that time
Although maybe it was a Wednesday.
The late comer, the beautiful, who has not gone with
    women,
Gets killed.
Why?
Is it jealousy of the virgin?

from *The Hen and the Bees* (1960)   101

Or fury at the virgin for suggesting that physical
        procreation is unnecessary?
But Baldar got into Valhalla all right
And feasts there still,
And Christ reached his Heaven
Of the many mansions
He was always talking about.
He'll have a wee house now there.
They both wanted that other kind of immortality
Not of the germ plasm
But of the spirit.
They both brought in the new unhappy split-up days,
Split-up ways,
Split-up-ness.
Baldar and Christ started that split un-nerving thing
        of the virgin male,
The idea of celibacy as a virtue,
The forcing of a choice between the spirit and the
        Flesh
As if there couldn't be both.
Both it must be.
Christ, you're wrong!
Baldar, you're hideous!

By the Book

Well, *why* should it all be down in a book?
– A Book!
How could it possibly be that someone else's
        revelation
Is more to go by
Than the inner revelation of oneself to oneself?
Words out of history
Are a legend living in us
But not the text.
They are for us to use, they are not to rule us.
It couldn't be that there's such a thing as a gospel
Written down once to serve for always.
It's there for recognising events by
But not for controlling their outcome,

Not for pushing at and shifting what happens
And making it seem only an illustration of the old
    thing.
Everything new has something to do with the old,
But it's not only that,
It's something new as well.
The book says
How it seems,
But it has to keep being said
In new ways
And it has to keep being seen
Differently.
There's no such thing as a book that serves as a
    text-book for all time.
There's no text-book of behaviour for our descendents.
There are no principles which are valid.
Each new moment is a new moment.

Sound of Children Sobbing

The children all cried aloud so desperately sadly
That it was useless to expostulate,
Hopeless to expect them to stop.
They had a grief of their own, deep in them,
And the courage to cry aloud with it.
Never in their lives again would they be allowed to
    cry like that,
So they cried,
And whoever heard them
Just knew
That it was true.

from *The Hen and the Bees* (1960)   103

Face-kicking

The boors
Are everywhere.
They kick you in the face.
Only in Scotland
Do those who love you kick you in the face.
They do it on purpose.
The feel they have to.
They feel they must
– For a valuable lesson, so they believe.
But we don't need the lesson.
We'd rather those who loved us just loved us.
We don't need the kicking in the face.

Facing page: Still from Where I Am Is Here *(1964), 'The Bravest Boat'.*
Courtesy of Scottish Screen Archive, National Library of Scotland /
copyright © Alex Pirie

Uncollected and Unpublished Poems

One is One

Then sing your song without me: I shall sing
Alone. But if by accident you hear,
Listen. – In every song of loss or Spring
Are overtones for the familiar ear.
The personal tries to speak to all, but those
Who love or loved us know what we would say.
The world may laugh in answer to our prose
Or weep for our sadness sung, as well it may;
Yet there remains the individual cadence
Which those who know us follow like a pulse.
For you my words have ultimate transparence,
As I in your rhythm feel my own impulse.
Dear, you must know I chiefly sing for you
In common language specialised for two.

(Summer 1950)

Studentessa (The Little Tourist in Rome)

Margaret sat on the steps of Spain
And ate a doughnut,
Wondering where should she go today.
Happily punctuating the steps
She sat and thought of where to go next
    – Say, the Vaticano?
Margaret going in purple and yellow
Climbed the steps in the early morning –
Life is good:
Why go and visit the tourist places?
Stay and watch the world go by
Halfway up the steps of Spain,
Out of the hot sun.

The tourists pass and so do the Romans.
Romans? Romans? Are these Romans?
What a name for the gentle people:
Is she a Roman this bambina
With a bunch of leaves in her fist, descending

Step by step with a fat soft matron?
Are they Romans the boys and girls
Arm in arm in the morning freshness,
And the idle youths with the elegant stride?

Here come the tourists, speaking German
Red and damp in the morning sunshine.
I am a tourist: so are they.
Soon I shall go to San Pietro.

Michelangelo Buonarotti
Fashioned a dome for the Roman cathedral.
Margaret going in yellow and purple
Gazed with the hundreds
At the dome that speaks of the glory of God.
Oh, admirable work of art:
    Say the tourists.
Pray for us, Mary, mother of God:
    Sing the pilgrims.

Lost in the rooms of Raffaello
Lost in the city's eternity
What became of the studentessa?
Did she shrink or did she grow?

Why in the world does the dottoressa
Masquerade as a studentessa?
So she can study without reproof
The gold in the street, the rose in the roof;
So she can be, without pretence,
A student, in the humblest sense.
So she went in her yellow shoes,
With all to gain and nothing to lose.

All was gain and growth,
She said.
By living, she grew.

(Summer 1950)

Uncollected and Unpublished Poems   107

The Window Boxes

Tramped on by the black stone
Poisoned by soot

Flowers in cities
Flags of flowers
Stuck in boxes
And forced to bloom.

I hate their brave
And concentrated look
Why not die?

Trampled thrusting
Coloured things
Stuck there
Stuck out at us.

Oh, flowers? Flowers!

Wild things, or
Garden things, – but this!

A wee box of barely
Adequate earth.
God, it's better to be
Cut and put in water.

Oh petals, sweet petals,
Soft petals
What a bashing to take!

(1957)

Seeing's Believing and Believing's Seeing

I don't have to know what it's all about.
That's not what I'm trying to know.
It's the looking that matters,
The being prepared to see what there is to see.
Staring has to be done:
That I must do.
I don't want to know why I do it
– I might *want* to know, but I know I'd never
          know that, no matter what –
But I know I have to look and look
And see what I can see
And the people I like are the people who look.
No matter what they see I like them looking.
There's a certain charm, though, in people who
          don't look *at all*.
They have innocence.
They have the real calm-eyed unseeing quality.
They accept everything, just everything
          everything everything
At any sort of value, maybe face value, they
          don't seem to mind.
They accept everything as being something else.
They don't *care* what it is, it's not that they
          pretend to know,
Or, rather, they just take it for what it seems
          to be but they just don't make a song about it;
          if you say it's something else they'll smile
          and say well it might be that too of course.
Well, if I was like that I could be like that.
But I can't pretend to be like that.
Being what I am, I have to look,
To stare and stare
And prod
And take apart,
Botanically detaching petals that maybe should
          be left alone
And roughly shattering things, too, to see
          what's there.
I have to stare at it all as it is
And I have to stare too at it all as it might be,

Which means undoing what it is, stopping it being
    what it is, so that it isn't there any more
        to stare at,
All so that I can stare at it the more,
Peer and probe into it.
God, it's endless what I want to do
    Have to do
    Go mad doing,
Turn mad mad mad at having always to do.

*

The reason I go on living is because I never win.
I lose, and continue.
Success is the end of trying.
Success is defeat.
Success wilts the spirit.
Success is the great discontent.

Ahimé! Ochone! Aloor!

You see now how I'm mad?
    – *Why*, I mean.

(7 November 1958)

Horses

It was a black horse she rode astride, bareback
when she was a child.
In the clouds
it was a white horse with mane of silver sheen
and polished hooves
which they gave to her later.
And she learned
to ride
side-saddle too, at times.
But there were still the times of bare knee-gripping
    mad rides across the waves and clouds
and at those times the mim white mare

galloped wildly ahead in very much the same way
as the black stallion of her childhood.

(7 November 1958)

Word Song

Words are the most delicate thing.
Words which can be picked up and set in place with a
pair of forceps.
The fingers are too gross.
Words passing through the air.
I catch them in handfuls.
One buzzed by my ear then.
They swarm around me
In my hair
And everywhere.
Spoken in different voices
Or lettered
I hear some word form a particular voice
Belonging to the voice that speaks it
And it's there too just as a word
Not in anybody's voice.
Words Change.
The voices change them
And you have to be careful which voice you catch them
      in and put them down in.
Only by careful earth of other words beside it, arranged
      and watered.
Do you get it to root
And, of course, shoot.
A word is not in the least like a plant
But the picking of words out and putting them hereabout
      thereabout
Is not unlike seed-sowing.
If you think about it like that, you can see it like that,
But it's not.
It is what it is, of course.

Oh and sometimes the words come crashing in
Bashing like waves at Yesnaby against the rocks
One after another
    Soar ——
       Crash!
Another
    Crash!
Lift, Crash!
    Up, wait, crash!
And at the very edge of that huge breaker in comes rushing,
    lightly, swiftly and daintily the very thing itself that is
    water.
The edge of the wave.

Sometimes words play games.
One will keep shouting itself in your ear
And then run away, when you turn round, run away repeat-
    ing and repeating and laughing.
Fix on it, and it seems there for no purpose
But it keeps coming back
And at last I really seize and hold it there and stare at it
And hold it to my ear,
Listen,
Rattle it,
Pull it apart letter by letter
And finally set it down.
Use it perhaps.

The way words have of turning themselves into song
Is one of their most endearing characteristics.
Even one word alone
Will go jigging along rhythmically.
To catch it I have to perform a sort of dance
And, beating about in the air as it does,
It links itself to other words.
Makes them sing too.
They all sing together.
Tra-la-lá, la-lá ....
But those are not words!
Words.
Listen

Published in *The Orkney Herald*, 11 November 1958

Poems, Stories and Writings

That's Them off on Their Spring Forays

The equinox excited the Vikings out of their winter stupor,
Made other lands seem desirable,
Made the roving sea and the turning world all a prod, a birch upon
    them, an unknown waiting welcoming motion to receive
    them:
And in they went
With the prows of their vessels high and proud,
Their weapons clanging against their shields,
With the swift sides of their long ships entering between two lips
    of water
And at speed rushing –
Yelling off to fight the Irish.
Off they went:
A voyage with life wagered, death won, by many of the company.

And what of Ingebjorg at home? is what I always think.
What of the women, digging, ploughing, sowing, reaping through
    the months of their pregnancy?
I always think of them –
With their men away all summer,
Fighting,
Raiding,
And the farm to mind, calves to rear, sheep to clip, the scanty grain
    to tend and harvest, ale to brew,
And a baby to be born.

The level day and night
Was too much for those exploring men
And the dream of the deepest sea in their eyes
Took them spinning down the coasts,
Ripping out into the ocean,
Conquering, drinking, raging, singing and composing verse
While they sought in the motion of all the earth and of the sea upon
    The earth,
(The sun's swing and the moon's swing and
The vivid gales and the flooding tide of the time of even days and
    nights),
Some secret
Or some prize.

I think of the women's eyes seeking too, as they waited,
In the movement which was all around them and within them
– Limbs stirring in the lower abdomen and lengthening of days –
Something else besides anything the men could bring home.

Published in *The Orkney Herald*, 13 January 1959

Drawing in Pen and Ink

Say it is from Ceylon
Or say it is from the Italian epoch
Or other recess.
Or say it was just there anyway.
Say I'm who I am and can't be otherwise.
Could I ever have NOT done the things I did?
I only ask myself that.
Nobody else can be expected to concentrate on
    Such a one-personed problem.
They have enough to do wondering about who *they* are,
What they are
And why,
And how it might have been otherwise if only
    things had turned out differently.

The pen, you see, came from Kandy
And the ink is an Edinburgh recollection
With overtones of what another person is to me
And to himself,
And is.
The person or even the thing connected is there
    Always inwardly ultimately and would be
    Connected no matter what I had ever done or
    Where ever been.

(3 March 1959)

The Sky of Your City

I've heard you say that that particular simultaneously
    intoxicating and thirst-quenching blue
Is the blue you remember for Edinburgh,
And in that blue is your love for your own city.
It's the deepest of all sky blues, the clearest,
    sorrowfulest – and yet joyous – calmest and most
    disturbing
Of any blue sky anywhere,
A deep unclouded – yet like pure cloud itself –
    essence of blue
Like a colour in your eyes which makes you seem
    yourself aerial, or celestial, at times.

(16 May 1959)

Why Did They Go?

The dust, the dust! Oh, Margaret, the dust, the dust.

My mother

Was it just
The endless fight against the dust
That made them flit from Skara Brae?

A necklace broke and fell,
Got covered in sand, and lay there,
Not at all that the population fled in terror,
Rather,
The labour of forever sweeping and cleaning was just
Too much,
Because, you see, the sand kept blowing in.

They sped.
They chucked it.
They vamoosed.
But was it any better where they went to?

I wouldn't have thought so.

The Raven Banner

If I had known you would be think-
    -ing to live forever,
      said Earl Sigurd's mother,
I would have brought you up in my
    woolbasket.

She made him a banner
To fight battles with.

The standard-bearer falls, always,
But the fight itself
Is strong as the raven standard,
Strong and ultimately telling as the
    fierce strong raven itself.

It is divinely unjust and inevitable
    that the carrier forward of the
    raven's inspiriting image must
    be killed.

Sigurd too fell in the end, carrying
    the standard.
That was Clontarf.

Published in *The Orkney Herald*, 2 February 1960

Concha Orcadensis

That black stooped form down in the ebb there,
      That's Robert Rendall.
He knows the place to find the shells.
I think he has a list of them all and can
      Identify them,
And in the whorled buckle he holds to his ear
Hears
Sea and messages,
Remarks of the trawlermen and the seals' bogle,
Swish and slosh and suck of the tide in the geo,

And the horrendous boom
In the under-rock cave,
Crabs crawling
And the sea-slaters discussing their interesting
     Ebb life
(Tired of the land, they are re-adapting for the sea)
And the soft water and the cry of the eider-chick,
The gentle falling of the sea over sand, harmonic ripple
     Of sea over sea,
The music where the burn enters
     – A little local tune –
And the distant movement of whales and of far ships.
He drops the familiar buckie or puts it in his pocket
And studies the clownish activities of bivalves
And notes what the great gale brought in,
Those miracles with names,
Those delicate masterpieces,
Those delights,
That rich material for study.

This Now

Ah no, this is it, this here, yes.
Now.
Don't miss it.
Don't just be absent, planning for the future
Or regretting the past.
But be.
Be here.
Be, now.

I always want everything to be now.
I'm no good at waiting.
I always want it all always happening.
I want my now now.

That's why I don't understand sacrifice.
Sacrifice makes no sense to me.
'Un po' di sacrificio.'
If it isn't any good now it isn't any good any time.

Free for All

In furnished rooms and Nissen huts
I pass my life being supervised
And, subject to the fuel cuts,
Accept the warmth that's offered me.
I take the bun that's proffered me,
Expecting neither more nor less,
And when I'm asked 'Do you agree?'
Obediently I answer 'Yes.'
I guard my mediocrity:
The universe is medium sized.

Flame

One day I
Lit a fire
At which I
Boiled eggs
Made tea
Dried my shoes
And I sat
On a stool
Watching
The sticks catch and flame
Quite a while
It seemed,
Until the whole pile I'd gathered had all burnt away.

Flame
Is a thing I
Always wonder about.
It seems to be made of colour only.
I don't know what else it's made of.

from *a twenty-seven-page 'Examination into the meaning of fire'*

I want to keep the light right here,
An element of life.
Light and heat *in* the life must not be let out, dispersed,
    burnt mushroom-high
Like an ending
With no phoenix.

There is nae movement in the warld like Hugh MacDiarmid's
    Circumjack Cencrastus,
But snakes don't really eat their tails.
They'd be mad if they did.
Snakes are not so silly.
Men have invented the devouring thing of destruction with
    no new beginning.
Fire without the phoenix,
Self-disintegration
Simply for the kicks.

Il Mago

I knew a magician in Perugia
who made medicines out of frogs' blood
and fabulous tonics for children
out of old iron.
He used to put the brew in a great pot
and stir it with an owl's feather.
The spells were spoken in Italian
with a French accent.
'Non trovi, mia cara? Io trovo.'
And the manufactured cardboard cartons
carried the pilula
(looking like any other pill you might buy anywhere)
into people's purses.
In the days of Mussolini he was prominent.
He is mentioned by Ezra Pound as a thinker.

Materfamilias

Me bairns all are born
Fae me heed and through me hand.
I ha'e no ither kind o' peerie babe
But only writings an bonny pictures.
I tak weel care o' them
And send them in the world wi' scrubbit faces,
An bid them tell the truth.

I've tried to gi'e them a grain o' the airs and graces
To mak their work lightsome
And so as the folk as meets them'll like them.

But wance they're oot o' me care
They ha'e their own life. I'll no interfere.
If they are strong and weel-made and honest
They'll mak oot theirsells.
If they are as I meant them a' to be
Their place is there for them.

A human sort of want might mak me think
That when I'm deed maybe they will recall
To folk as kent me
Familiar tones of voice half minded on
A glance or tone of voice.

Me

The germ plasm continues
While neighbours come and go.
In me no, though.
In me it came to a stop.
Sometimes it comes to a stop.
Well, perhaps it's predestined that all my energy
          Has to be used for other things than direct
          Continuation of my own line of inheritance –
Perhaps,
Oh, how can I know if what I do with all this me
          That there is is what I was meant to do?

How can I know?
I can't know.
All that I might have devoted to my children
Is devoted outwardly, oh, to everybody,
And inwardly, to me, to know me, know myself so
        Far as I can tell about myself.

Something has to change, for women.
It's not right as it is just now, between men
                        And women.
I have to use myself and peer into myself and
        Try to find out what it *is* about women.
I *have* to.
My life has to be used for this.
Some old witch or some old godmother was present
                        At my christening.

There's a legendary quality in all this.

One must recognise one's own legend
When it comes.
The story of you and me
Was told some centuries ago
But isn't over.

It will be told again and again.

In Olden Days

Spectators at a hanging
Felt
– Safe, perhaps?
They watched.
They stood there, craning to watch a death.
In a chattering crowd they went away
After the hush.
But the hush, for a dangling body with a dropped head, was
        continuous,
Not broken and not ever to be broken by the relieved murmur,
The excited laugh of having witnessed too much.

Uncollected and Unpublished Poems   121

People watched death then
As a spectacle.
They saw the last moment, shame and extinction together.
It wasn't themselves, it was someone else,
But it was someone.
The excuse they had for not being perturbed was that the person up
    There was a criminal.
They ordered the killing
And they watched it.
It was logical.

Winter Solstice

The world is reeling out to its very utmost once again
Until it must shudder to stop and turn
And let the light back to us,
Back into the lower dark storeys and the foot of the valleys.
It is revolving in the darkest possible way now for us in the North,
And the time of all-light is half a year away.

What is it that's wonderful about the photograph?

    ——.
    ——.
    You can see the tide going down the sound.
    You can see the slack, not in the stream of
                the current.
    You can see the swell at the shore making
                waves break.
    And none of it at all turbulent.
    All of it calm with the calm of a calm day,
    Only, even in the calm the current is strong
    And you see this reflected in small wave
                movements on the surface;
    And in the photograph these little wave shadows
            Seem to lead from the left to the right.
    The motor boat is moored just this side of the
                current in easier water

And the dinghy being pushed off by the two men
        standing up in it
Makes a circle of disturbed water in where
        rising waves come in
Which the tide going either in or out –
And I can only tell which because I know the
        place: the tide is coming *in*, I see, because
        the current in the stream is from the west to
        east through Calf Sound –
Sends washing on the rocks at slowed-down
        blood-beat intervals.

(9 June 1962)

The Boats at Droman

These boats are like the Viking ships.
They are like the Westray skiffs.
They are like the Eday boats.
They are like the Orkney yol.

They are shaped as if the sea had smoothed them into that shape.

These boats are like the ancient Viking ships, but not so big.
They are not so broad in the beam, not so dipped in the side, not
        so long of course, not so big as the long ships were.
The same shape is in them, the same curving of timbers, the same
        breadth to take the sea, the same swift appearance, the beauty.
They look narrow and pointed because of the sharp stern and the
        sharp bow; but they are not narrow in the beam, they are
        quite wide.
Nine long boats and three smaller ones, hauled up high on the grass.

The houses are like rocks or like plants in the ground, but the
        boats are like living animals and very strong.
They are built for sail, and yet
Those that are used at all have engines in them now.
Then some there in the line when you get near you see they are
        unpainted, dry, and gaping in places, the boards have
        sprung, they have been left for too long.

It is past the days for these long heavy strong beautiful
         boats. There are not the men to man them, they are
         uneconomical, they aren't the right boats anymore, there are
         other boats.

The new boats are broad, bigger with more of a rake from stem to
         stern, with decking, with a cabin and wheelhouse, built to go
         far out to sea and stay out all night.
The new boats have to be more powerful and more safe,
But the hulls that accommodate engines still are like boats on
         the Norwegian coast, are like Orkney boats.

A story gets told in Gaelic, in Greek, in Breton, in Welsh, in
         German and Persian, the same story with different characters
but with recognisable events and the same detailed incidents.

The boats at Droman might be used for a day at the lobsters. They
might be returned to with a great feeling of pleasure. It would be
pointless to try and make your living from them entirely. It might
be useless to think even with that and crafting you could live. It is
not enough now. People want more. You can't do it by yourself.
         So I don't exactly weep for the boats at Droman, although they
give me a feeling of something fine and sure that has been lost.
         I can't keep away from them. I keep walking down to look at
them. (The pier is on the Ordnance map.)

How can I not just leave them there and forget about them? People
died and left them. People drove away and left them. People took
ships to America and left them. People flew off in aeroplanes and
left them. People stayed around and worked the land, learnt
mechanical engineering, bought their food at the van and left the
boats, didn't build anymore, didn't need anymore new ones, left
them there hauled up above the shore, at hand for a day or two at
lobsters in harvest time.

(22 April 1966)

Redefinition of a Lame Duck

for Hugh MacDiarmid on his eightieth birthday

In a pub, I watched two blind men
Separately getting drunk.
One, a student, had scars where glass exploded in his face, once.
Once was enough: look, no eyes!
His friends are enjoying his quips about his state.
'He's great. He jokes about it.'
'Drink up!' Engendering love, he drinks up.
He generates warmth, as does
The powerless Highlandman offering drams
– The cork of the bottle goes straight in the fire –
The wild Lewisman shielding the secret of the bothans
– He mumbles his name, but straightens up proudly to regale
    the Court with a rigmarole of lies –
And the shrewd Orkneyman, who, tilting up a half-bottle, remarks,
    'They say we're dyin' oot.'
The plump son of the other one pushes a pint along the bar,
'Here you are, Daddy.' He needed that:
He doesn't find his blindness funny.
        And then see those
        Very black glasses
    Must be protecting a glimmer, some remnant of sight.
'We are all lame ducks here,' the politician said,
'We are all lame.'
And we're all blind together, we'll all fry together,
We're all drunk together when we're drunk, drunk, drunk,
Together, blind drunk together, when, together, boys, together, eh!
Eh, no?
We are the people, wee wee pawky people
And god help you lot
When
Us yins
Ge' a drink in us.
'Here you are, Daddy.' 'Thanks, son.'
'Here you are, Son.' 'Thanks, Daddy.'
        Maybe, maybe, maybe,
        Lord God Almighty!
We need our poets, like MacDiarmid here
Who has kept blowing on and even made to glow sometimes
The small spark of life that is still in us as a nation.

(1972)

Orquil Burn

A poem started in words goes on in the picture; part of quite
another (finished) poem is read for the last of the nine. Out of my
own memory and thought, I find the external scenes to make a
picture from.

A burn in the Orkney Isles is followed
                          all the way from its last
                                    waterfall over the
                    sea banks at Scapa
            past distillery and farms
                          under bridges and
                    over waterwheels, through
        its man-made diversions
            and natural
        vagaries to its
            source
        among the heather.
        Flowers by the banks,
            boys sailing boats,
                    animals on the farm
            and the everlasting
        dance and music of the water itself
                                    are the stars.

Soon

Things don't end: things begin.
Everything is a beginning,
A racing
On and on and on.

Oh! How my chest aches!
How I gasp for enough air!

That's all that's there.

The last poem written by the character Greta
in *Blue Black Permanent* (1992)

Grove

Is a holy place
Calmly looked at for what it is.
It is as it should stay.
Although of course
Nothing and nowhere stays as it is
… so that the particular time
of the grove being seen –
our view of it, the feeling about it,
and the sounds heard there
all have a
there and then and never again quality.

(February 1998)

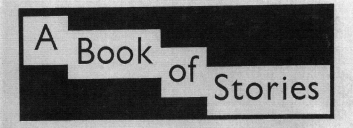

lane furniture

A Book of Stories

Margaret Tait

'I think it's marvellous,' he pronounced. 'It's a wonder nobody ever noticed it before.'

'There's a sort of *thing* about it,' she agreed, 'a real thing. I don't know.'

'That's what I meant,' he said.

The boatman looked at his two passengers appraisingly, as an automatic exercise in human assessment, not because those were particularly interesting. They had been a bit stingy in what they had offered him to take them over to the island, especially since he had meant to go fishing (and he heard there were good fish out-by these last days). But he took them of course. It would be altogether too churlish to refuse, and perhaps they were really poor and needed the free lift.

The girl whispered to her husband, glancing sideways at the boatman, 'It's rather sweet the way he's so proud to be taking us over.'

The young man's beard blowing in the wind caught his laugh of sudden joy, his expression of abrupt realisation of his own power.

'A bit off his head maybe,' thought the boatman, 'like many of those folk from the south.'

'I like him,' said the young man to his wife. 'Our boatman is a personality.' He glanced benevolently at the boatman.

'I know, dear, you do like people like that,' said the young wife, proudly, 'strange people.'

'What sort of age will they be, now?' The boatman considered to himself, his eyes watching the buoy ahead and discerning too the breaking of the roost beyond the island. He looked at the pair quickly, observantly. 'About thirty,' he decided, 'or maybe thirty-five. Not so young as I first thought. I wonder what they earn their living at, dressed like that.'

The man was addressing him. 'Has anyone ever been to the island before?' he asked.

What could the man mean? What on earth could the man mean?

'Today, you mean?' asked the boatman, quite puzzled. The wife giggled, and hugged her husband's arm.

'No, I meant *ever*,' said the man.

'It's a very favourite place for summer picnics,' explained the boatman, 'especially for people from hereabouts, you know. The visitors from away don't always get to it. It's an interesting island, though. I knew it fine when I was a boy, for my grandfather had a croft there. There were four farms there then, but now it's uninhabited.'

'Oh, was it once inhabited?' they both asked eagerly, thinking of the uncultured remoteness of life in such a place.

'Just imagine!' the wife exclaimed. 'I knew there was a thing about it.'

They both stared at the island.

'I love small boats,' she said. 'They're so *exciting*.'

'An exciting *shape*,' said her husband. 'I'm glad we came here.'

'I think we can really do something with this,' she said. 'It gives me *ideas*.'

'We'd need a whole new form,' he said, grandly sweeping the air with one hand. 'I'd have to work it out of course. But it's for me. It's as if it had all been waiting for me to come.'

Her eyes danced as she matched the movement of the boat with her body's balance.

'Might make a sailor in time,' thought the boatman, 'although they were hopelessly clumsy climbing in.'

He landed them on the island, helping them on to the rocks, with a warning about the slippery seaweed. They staggered, slipping, up towards the dry rocks and grassy slope above, laughing gaily when they got their feet wet. They had agreed to be left there for two hours. The little boat put out again. The boatman had a line to drop, so that his afternoon might not be entirely wasted.

'Oh look!' she exclaimed, '… at the boat. Isn't it exciting.'

The sturdy yawl, the little boat of resolute seaworthy shape, carried the boatman who guided it to the edge of the tideway where he hoped to haul in a few haddocks. His boat earned him a living, and she was like a sort of garment or home to him too. The day he got her home all the neighbours had gathered to see the latest masterpiece from the builder. 'My, did you ever see such a bonny stern,' his friend Sinclair exclaimed at once. 'That stern now!' said the quiet old man from the waterside. 'Look at the stern, boys. It'll take the sea, that one.' The boatman owner was proud to hear those comments and knew they were sound. His boat was built to weather the sea, and a boat-builder's eye for beauty and purpose had determined its lines.

Those people on the island! He hoped they wouldn't go and get lost or fall over a cliff or anything. Visitors did daft things in their ignorance sometimes. It was lightsome to have visitors and to see the different ones coming, though many were a bit odd, like those two. They didn't seem ever to have seen anything before. Poor souls, perhaps they had been all their lives in a city street. It was nice for them to be having a change – so long as the weather kept good. People liked to come and enjoy the sunshine and the quiet. 'The visitors maybe even enjoy the scenery better than we do who live here,' he laughed to himself. 'Nice to see people coming and appreciating your own place. Most of them don't think it's a place to live in, though. We can have it, for them.'

'Boys, boys, just the weather to-day for a fine catch. I hope the boy's managing. I could have been out there fine, all day.' Nuisance really, having to take those two over, but he didn't refuse. The wife said he had no business sense and just *liked* showing off the place to people. 'Everybody can't be expected to feel for it the way we do,' she'd say, 'we who live and die here and get our living out of the place and watch the weather because of what it does to us.' 'I like people to like it,' was all he could reply… But today, well, to-day he really would rather have been fishing, not in this half-hearted way in the nearest place handy but away where he knew it to be best on such a day.

The man and woman walked across the island turf. It was springy and made walking like flying as the wind sang past them and some inquisitive birds swept alarmingly close to their heads.

'We'd better just decide to stay,' she said.

'I like it,' he said. 'I could make something of it.'

'It'll be great,' she said, 'a wonderful thing. We'll really put it on the map, you know, really you know.'

'Yes,' he said. He was smiling at the broad horizon he saw before him.

'Oh, look at that shape!' she exclaimed. 'That big rock. Isn't it marvellous.'

'Oh yes,' he said, 'come on.'

They scrambled over the rocks to gaze up at a looming crag standing out from the shore like a separate island. 'Oh look,' he said, 'it's quite easy to climb it on the other side – and we could get across by those stones.'

There was a connecting chain of flat rocks sticking out of the sea and it was an easy matter to clamber across to the base of the crag and then climb up its sloping, grassy side.

At the top they lay on their bellies and peered over the cliff at the birds clamouring on the ledges below. Hundreds of long-necked cormorants stood in rows along the lowest rocks near the sea and others of them were swimming and diving. The two people lay and stared down at the swirling water and at the raucous birds taking it all for granted. A young fulmar sat trembling in a bare nest on a ledge quite close to them, but they did not see it. The wheeling gulls and fulmars and quick puffins kept up their hypnotic motion, endlessly it appeared. The man and woman were not aware of the time passing, but only of the magnificence of their surroundings and of their own future.

'I love doing things that are *different*,' she said, 'I wonder if anyone has ever been here before.'

It was a clear day and the distant land rising serenely out of the ruffled water was visible in unusual detail.

'It's like battleships,' he said, and she said, 'No. I see it like needlework, like something delicate.'

'Do you?' he asked her. 'They don't see it at all. It's lucky we came here.'

Out beyond they saw the boat turn and come back toward the island. They stood up and waved to the boatman, and then began to clamber back the way they came.

The boatman saw them on the Scarfie Rock and his heart softened to them. They were just like everyone else. Nobody can ever resist going out on the Scarfie Rock. He as a small boy staying with his grandfather had visited it almost daily.

They were walking along the shore parallel to the boat coming in. 'He's coming back early,' the man said. 'I suppose he sort of missed us, out there by himself.'

At the landing place, he leapt into the boat with gay exuberance, and nearly cupped it. She then followed, with the helping hand of the boatman to steady her, and shortly they left the island.

They saw his fish. 'Will you eat all those at home?' they asked.

'Oh no,' he said, 'I'll sell them in the town. I would have been out past to-day,' he said, not exactly regretfully, but thinking about it. 'My son will be out for fish, out there.' He pointed to the open sea.

'Oh, fishing,' they said, identifying the activity.

'What did you find on the Scarfie Rock?' asked the boatman.

'Scarfie Rock?'

He pointed to where he meant.

'Oh, has it got a name?' the man asked. 'We climbed on to it. There's a sort of line of rocks and you can just get across if you jump over the last bit. You should go there some time.'

'Aye. I ken it,' said the boatman.

'It's wonderful there. There are so many birds, especially ones with long necks, sort of black, or dark grey.'

'Scarfies,' said the boatman, 'cormorants.'

'We'll look them up in the book when we get back,' said the wife, not having understood what the boatman said. 'We think it's wonderful,' she confided. 'We're going to write about it. We're both writers. What did you call the rock?' she said. 'You should go there some time. It's marvellous really, and you can go over great boulders just like stepping-stones.'

'Aye, you can about walk across to it at low tide,' said the boatman.

Published in *Lane Furniture* (1959)

'You should ask old William Garson,' Jeanie said to Mr Joseph MacBayne, the folk-song collector. 'He knows a lot of the old songs.'

'William Garson?' said Joseph. 'Where does he live?'

'Come here to the door,' said Jeanie, 'and I'll show you.'

Joseph went to the door and looked across the sparkling fields. The huge sky seemed to take up more room here than elsewhere, and even the intensely blue ocean which beat against the west shore of the island was diminished in comparison.

'Look,' said Jeanie. 'See that two-storied house over there; and then to the left of it there's a cottage, with a peat stack. That's Wiliam Garson's.

'What would be a good time to find him in?'

'He'd be there now. He doesn't go far, these days.'

Joseph arranged with Jeanie that he would come back to the farm for his tea. Then he gathered up his portable sound recorder and a few other things that he needed, and set off along a thyme-scented old grassy road. Half a mile down the brae, cars and lorries and vivid red postal vans ambled past, and the sound of their engines mixed with the sound of the bees in the thyme into a general summery buzz. The long line of the road below shimmered bluish-black and tarry in the sun, but the grassy road was soft and cool to walk on.

Joseph wore a kilt dyed with the correct ancient dyes for the tartan of his family. The tweed of his jacket was woven by Hebridean weavers from wool spun by crofters. The leather buttons on it had been hand-tooled for him specially by an old craftsman he had discovered working in a tiny shop in Fortrose. To support him on his journey he carried a handsome shepherd's crook the exquisite carving of which had been done by last year's first prize-winner at the Royal Highland and Agricultural Show.

William Garson saw him coming, and his curiosity was so aroused by the strange figure in the familiar landscape that when the meticulously dressed gentleman – a visitor from some town, no doubt – came towards his own cottage a warm smile of welcome and gratification lit up his wrinkled old face.

'Aye,' said William, when Joseph came level with him, 'it's a fine day.'

'It is that,' said Joseph; then he paused, to let the old man conduct the introduction in his own way.

'You'll be a photographer,' said William, eyeing Joseph's equipment. 'You're getting grand weather for photographing.'

'No,' said Joseph. 'I take sounds, not pictures.'

'Is that right?' said William, and he had a good look at the paraphernalia slung around Joseph's person, but of course there was not much to see, because the protecting cases concealed what was inside.

'Are you William Garson?' said Joseph. 'I hear you know some old songs.'

'William Garson's the name,' said William. 'Pleased to meet you.' He held out his hand.

Joseph shook hands. 'I'm Joseph MacBayne,' he said, and he paused to see if the old man recognised his name. 'You may have heard of me,' he said.

'No,' said William, 'no, I can't say I have. But we don't hear about everybody up here. We're not so greatly affected by what goes on in the towns, you ken. Songs, you said. It's only the old ones I ken, though. I'm no weel up in what the young folks sing nowadays.'

'It's the old ones I'm after,' said Joseph.

'There's nothing quite like the old songs,' said William Garson. 'That hill-billy stuff the young chaps play is all right too, but I like the old Scotch ones best.'

'So do I,' said Joseph. 'Of course hill-billy is derived from genuine old folk-song too, although *here* it's an import.'

'Aye,' said Wiliam. 'It's old too, is it? I don't mind it in me young days, but maybe I wasna hearing everything.'

By this time William had really taken in the fact that the visitor had come down the grassy road specially to call on him, and he felt very flattered. In these parts the kilt was like a strange foreign garment, so seldom was it seen, except when the Pipe Band was out, on gala occasions, and William liked too Mr MacBayne's proper way of speaking and he tried to prune his own accent to what the visitor would understand.

'You'll no fairly mak oot what we're saying sometimes,' William laughed.

'I have a good Scotch tongue in my head too,' said Joseph, slightly piqued.

'Aye,' said William. 'You speak more proper over there in the Mainland. We have our own Speech here in the islands.'

'I can follow most of the local dialects,' said Joseph.

'Do you smoke?' asked William, as he was filing his pipe. 'I can give you a fill.'

When Joseph took out his pipe, William had to admire it, for it was a very beautiful piece of work.

Joseph passed some hours at William's cottage, and recorded a number of songs. They were interesting variants of songs found on the Scottish mainland, but there was nothing which seemed intrinsically local in origin, and Joseph felt that this time he had made no great discovery. The old man remembered the words amazingly well, and his diction, as he sang in a clear but cautious voice, was precise and sure. The day was warm, it was delightful to hear the old man singing, and Joseph genuinely loved the tunes themselves. He could have gone on and on recording, but he had rationed himself to a certain length of tape, so as to leave some for the evening when he had another session at the farm-house. After that, he would return to Glasgow and sort out what he had collected in his latest tour.

Joseph admired old William's technique at the microphone. 'Anyone would think you'd done this all your life,' he laughed.

William laughed too. 'No all me life,' he said. 'But there have been folk here before, from the BBC, and then some others for a television film. They wanted the old songs too.'

Singing all afternoon was quite hard work for the old man, and he was all for making a cup of tea for the pair of them. But Joseph had promised Jeanie that he would be back for tea, and he knew that she had baked specially, so, regretfully, he had to decline the old man's offer of a genial cup with him.

When Joseph had hitched his equipment back on his shoulders and gone away, back up the grassy road, William watched him for a while, and waved when he turned round, and then he went into his house and made his own tea, for himself.

After tea at the farm, Joseph met the people whom Jeanie had asked to come and play and sing for him. A silent young man played fiddle tunes, and Joseph recorded one or two he had not heard before, reserving judgment meantime on their origin. The young man had learnt them from his grandfather, who had been a famous fiddler in the parish after he retired from a long active life at sea. The young man said he believed his grandfather made some of them up himself.

Most of the tunes they played and sang were well-known Scotch ones, but the rhythm had been changed slightly.

'Those tunes are heard all over the mainland too,' Joseph told them, 'only you don't play them as correctly. I mean, compared with the *original* way, your beat is wrong, just slightly out somehow. It's queer.'

And he got them to play over for him again an old reel that he loved but which had been transmuted into something else, recognisable and yet different, and although he tried to be detached and scientific about it, this other way of playing his favourite jarred on him.

'I always liked the Scotch songs,' said Jeanie. 'Better maybe than what the bairns get at school, though they're nice too, – you know, like I Shot an Arrow In the Air, A Brown Bird Singing, Drink To Me Only. Most of us who went to music got those. It was all written-down songs. My grandmother was a very bonny singer, and so was my Aunt Jane. She had her voice trained, and it was Italian opera songs she sang.'

'It's a pity,' said Joseph. He wondered whether there never had been any song there or whether it had all been lost at a time before scholars thought of saving such things.

Joseph had the songs he had taken from country people in other parts of the country magnetically registered on lengths of tape. These he would carry back to the city, where he knew that people would be charmed by the simple country songs which he preserved in this valuable work of his. So now, even if the country folk lost their songs the city society would have them instead, not inside themselves as generations of land peasants had had them and handed them on, but outside, on gramophone records, on tape, to be bought or not bought according to the desire of the moment and the money available, to be listened to with a critical ear, classified, compared with similar material from elsewhere, to be stored up by the genuinely musical ones and used again perhaps in different ways.

'I've heard of an old lady in one of the smaller islands,' said Jeanie, 'long ago though – she's dead now – who sang out a whole lot of verses to the minister exactly word for word what's in one of the old sagas. The minister was a learned man and he knew about it. But that was long ago.'

'Interesting,' said Joseph.

'The young folk get their songs from the wireless now,' said one old woman. 'They all do this American crooning. It's bonny too, some of it.'

'Peerie Mansie's right good at it,' said Jeanie. 'Have you heard him?'

Joseph MacBayne smiled as tolerantly as he could. He had

heard the rustic crooning too, and the clumsy aping of sophisticated slickness had offended him deeply.

'Will we play you the one we played on the wireless last year?' asked the fiddler who led the group in playing. 'It was made up specially by Jimmy here.'

'Yes, please,' said Joseph.

So they played.

'That was wonderful,' said Joseph. 'Now, why don't the local wireless fans copy *that*?'

'Too near home, I suppose,' said the fiddler.

'It puts folk off to hear themselves on the wireless,' said Jeanie. 'Nobody wants to be an old relic for professors to come and study.'

'They like to be in the swing,' said the old woman who had spoken before. 'They want what's new.'

'But that's new,' said Joseph, 'if it was only written last year.'

'Oh, aye, in a way,' said the old woman.

'Would that be a folk tune?' asked Jeanie. 'I always hear them talking about folk music, on the wireless, but what exactly does it mean?'

'It's the ancient music of the people,' said Joseph.

'Only the *ancient* music?' asked Jeanie. 'Is there never any new?'

'Not often nowadays,' said Joseph.

'If folk play it, that disna mak it folk music,' a man said. 'The folk play all sorts o bruck noo.'

'Well maybe we can change the American eens to wur own way,' said the old woman, 'same as Mester MacBaye says we changed the Scotch wans.'

'What we hear on the wireless,' said Jeanie, 'is only some London folk's idea of jazz anyway. Some Americans staying here last year said it was no very good. But they fairly laughed when they heard Jock o the Myres at it. That was worse still.'

'Oh, all that's quite a different thing,' said Joseph. 'It's city stuff. It's all done for the money in it.'

'We hev to get wur songs fae some piece,' said the old woman, 'or make them up wursells, for we haena any folk music.'

'Yes, it's sad,' said Joseph.

He felt a nostalgia for the parts of the country where the ancient ways were preserved, where he would be sure of finding some almost obsolete craft or custom still in use and the old songs still being sung, awaiting only such a one as him to carry away a specimen or a recording for the interest and delight of the great centres. Here, there was really nothing. The beauty of the islands received his heartiest admiration, but one couldn't live on that. Even the farming methods were up-to-date, calmly scientific and prosperous, the ancient inhabitants would talk to a stranger about world politics and the prospects for the crops in Australia rather than tell him old folk tales, and the shops sold manufactured goods. In the country, Joseph preferred people to be really countrified. If you had to be civilised, he thought, you might as well be civilised properly, and he would be glad to get back to Glasgow.

(3 July 1956)

Sixteen Frames per Second

The little boy stared and stared at the immense silent hooves on the screen above him, and although he was about dropping with sleep he couldn't take his eyes off them. Beside him, his mother played away resoundingly on the upright piano. He knew the music she was playing as intimately as he knew his mother's own moods and could almost tell by the way she played just what story he would have at bed-time and certainly whether she would be loving and dilatory or brisk and rather distant as she sometimes was.

The mother was entirely taken up in her adult and exacting occupation, and so the little boy was quite alone, related neither to the immense spectres on the screen nor to the jolly crowd out there, all facing the screen and laughing up at it as they followed the pranks of images they knew. He was in between, and could watch either as he chose. Usually he chose to watch the grey abstractions rather than the smelly, laughing, coughing humans in rows beyond the balustrade and the pot plants.

One night, though, he had watched a little boy rather younger than himself who sat in the very front row between his handsome young parents. The boy was young to be out for an evening's entertainment, and really it appeared as if he might have been taken along only because the parents wanted to be there and could not leave him at home alone. At first he sat in his own seat, frowning a little at the incomprehensible figures on the screen, and playing at tipping his seat up by changing his posture. This was found very irritating by the lady behind him, who, after a time, put a stop to it, and then the child slumped lower and lower until his father took him on his knee, and there he fell soundly asleep.

The little boy beside the piano watched the other child, who slept on his father's knee unaware of the two conflicting realities present in the theatre, much as he himself felt outside them. All through the picture he looked and looked at the boy comfortably asleep in his father's arms, supported rather as he was supported by his mother's nearness and by the steady beat of the music which she performed so sturdily.

The memory of the sleeping child among the audience did give the little boy beside the piano a dim sort of realisation that out there in that crowd which he heard and smelt but only dimly saw there must be others like himself. But being himself isolated where he was it did not occur to him that he might meet and know those others.

Poems, Stories and Writings

The wild white horse on the screen had broken out of the stockade once again, and went galloping away over the hills quite out of reach of its pursuers. The little boy then watched the giant grey figures of cowboys discussing what they would do next, and their words too appeared in gigantic letters rather too much at a slant from where he sat for him to be able to read them. The cowboys' horses were very beautiful too, but they had just been saddled and were setting out into the hills when a strange flickering took place, and blurred figures rushed vertically up the screen and into nothing. Then they stopped, and there was darkness.

For a moment his mother hesitated, then she went on playing jog-trot music for about a half a minute until the lights went up.

It was like lighting a match in a cave and finding it full of people. They stretched, and moved in their seats, and many of them laughed at the physical surprise of the breakdown and then the lights. They mostly kept staring fixedly towards the screen for a few moments, but presently a general chattering began and got louder and louder. The girls selling popcorn came down the aisles and there was even a sort of joviality about the interruption.

The little boy's mother had stopped playing when the lights went on, but the manager came from a private door down near the screen and told her to play something as it would take a few minutes to put things right in the projection room. She started on some popular songs of that time, and although at first the music could hardly be heard above the hubbub of talk there were a few in the crowd who listened and even joined in with their voices. She played a hit song, and very soon the packed auditorium was filled with the not entirely tuneful singing of all those people.

The little boy, who had been examining the blankness of the screen with a certain sort of interest, turned then to watch the other spectacle, of the audience. His mother played away vivaciously, for it was stimulating for her to find the audience actually paying attention to her music. During the films she sometimes wondered if they noticed her playing at all, although of course they would notice if she stopped. So now she played the popular songs extraordinarily well, reacting to the enthusiasm of the listeners and the singers. The little boy watched the people singing, rows and rows of wide open mouths and swaying shoulders. One joker even got into the aisle and 'conducted' them with flourishes of his arms.

At the end of the song there was a tremendous applause. The manager reappeared.

'Something quieter,' he said. 'Play something quieter.'

So the little boy's mother played a simple, rather sentimental tune, but one that the audience could hardly be expected to know the words of. Some stalwarts tried to sing it all the same, but the glorious unison of the popular song was gone for ever and a certain restlessness made itself felt among the crowd. There was a shuffling of feet and an occasional cry of 'Hurry up, there,' and 'What are we waiting for?'

One little family was so grateful for the joyous song in which all the house had taken part that they came down the aisle and leaned across the balustrade to thank the pianist. She was quite touched and just continued playing rather softly and absentmindedly while she talked to them. The little boy tried to keep behind the piano and not be seen by the well-dressed lady and gentleman and by the almost grown-up boy and girl.

'You haven't got your little boy with you tonight,' said the lady. 'You know, we often see you together, outside, and the children say, "There goes the wee boy from the picture-house, with his mother." But I suppose he's home in bed now.'

'No, he's here,' said the mother. 'Where are you?' So the little boy had to come out and be seen.

'I do believe you were hiding,' said the lady, laughing roguishly. 'But I have something here for little boys who *aren't* hiding.' And from her ample handbag she produced a box of sweets.

'Oh mother!' said the girl.

'Be quiet,' said the lady. 'We'll get more.' And she handed the box to the little boy, who just gazed at it in dismay.

'Take it,' said the gentleman. 'They're sweets. Perhaps you don't like sweets, eh? Ha ha ha.'

'You take them for him, then,' the lady said to the little boy's mother. 'He's shy.'

'He's sleepy,' said his mother. 'Thank you very much, but you shouldn't do this.'

'We really appreciate your playing,' said the lady's husband.

'Say thank you,' the little boy's mother said to him.

'Thank you,' said the little boy.

'There now, that's a good little boy,' said the lady.

The lights gave a warning flicker.

'We'd better get back to our seats,' said the big boy.

'Yes, hurry,' said the girl.

'We'll see you again, sonny,' said the lady, as they all went away.

The man turned and waved to him, and he waved back, but he felt his security jangled and he hoped that his own secret situation by the piano would never again be invaded by people from the audience. It was as unfitting for that to have happened as it would have been for the black and grey figures from the screen to jump down beside him.

Then the picture started again, and his mother played trotting music as the cowboys rode over the hill, and now and again when the little boy glanced nervously towards the audience he was relieved to see that all the people were safely hidden in darkness.

Published in *Lane Furniture* (1959)

WRITINGS ON FILM

Time

This morning I spent two and three-quarter hours taking stop-motion pictures of escholtzia opening, making one exposure every minute. I started at 13 mins to 8 when the flowers were still practically closed, set up the camera put a clock and exposure meter nearby, finished at 10.30 am. During this time I was living by minutes. I learned a lot about how much one can do in a minute, for between clicks I made my breakfast, ate it, cleared it away, read a letter from Daddy, read a bit of the newspaper.

I found that if I clicked the shutter then walked into the house to the kitchen, took the coffee pot out of the cupboard and filled it with water and set it down, then returned to the camera, the minute was up. In the next minute I went in, took the coffee tin from the shelf, put several spoonfuls in the appropriate part of the percolator, replaced the tin. Next minute, put the inside into perc., set it on the stove and switched on. And so on.

Some minutes I just stood by the camera and almost *felt* the time going by, *participated* in the flowers opening. I was especially conscious of the character of the light minute by minute. Characteristics of time and lighting would bring a feeling of essentially similar atmosphere elsewhere – Orkney, Dal Lake, and so on. There was a particular feeling of identification of place with place and participation because of the exactness with which I was observing the time passing. Watching the light acutely because of my exposure for one thing.

I remember how determined I was some time in my childhood to really *see* the clover closing up, feeling sure that if I kept on looking I couldn't fail to see, and being disappointed because I never did but putting it down to the fact that I never had the patience to keep on watching, not perceiving how the movement could be imperceptible.

*

(Cf. T.S. Eliot 'I have measured out my life in coffee spoons.' !)

Incidentally, the piece of film exposed was not satisfactory. I think more than once a minute would have been better.

(4 July 1949)

On Rossellini

I asked Rossellini just what they meant when they say that he shoots his films without a shooting script. He says he doesn't put his sceneggiatura [screenplay] down in writing but that he has it very clear in his mind. He thinks that producers have you by the ear when they have your sceneggiatura written down in so many words – so in order to preserve his liberty he doesn't write a sceneggiatura. But he investigates the ambiente [environment] the type of personaggio etc. very thoroughly, he says for many months and then when his characters come alive in his mind he constructs in his mind the sequences and the sequence of sequences which is his film. He makes a few written notes on this, but not in great detail.

Then the signora in charge of the attori attrici [actors, actresses] intervened wanting to introduce Giulia, the bambina and went on for about 10 mins about the 'Brava bambina, bravissima giovane attrice, ha il teatro nel sangue' [A good little girl, a very good young actress, she's got the theatre in her blood] etc.

When Rossellini came back to the subject there was by then a crowd wanting to hear him and his discourse wavered a bit especially as new people kept coming along and asking the original question again. Whether he thinks he would do better with a written script provided it didn't menace his liberty, I don't know.

(February 1951)

Portrait of a Lady in a Green Dress

'Portrait of a Lady in a Green Dress'.

no –

'Portrait of my Mother in a Green Dress'.

or simply 'My Mother in a Green Dress' or 'The Green Dress'.

The 2nd is the best. Indicates too *how* it is to be looked at. I think the audience probably needs a clue like that.

Related to painting.

For this film I am using a different method of editing. Instead of cutting the whole footage into shots and hanging them up or putting them in tins then joining together in a preconceived or else trial way, I looked quite thro the lot several times until 2 or more shots suggested themselves as going together. I then went thro it on the moviola, took out the shots I wanted to see together and *only* them, joining up the spaces they came out of.

In the first cut for instance I took out five shots only – one group of three and one of two. I joined them up in the way that had occurred to me, putting a bit of tail between the two groups, and looked at it. The 'kitty' was still all joined up too, so then I looked at all of it again. Something didn't work in the first choice, so I took it out and put it back in the kitty. And so on. Gradually building up the film roll and gradually reducing the kitty but *all* of the material being at *all* times projectable. Never anything left lying in tins so that I couldn't see what it was.

This is a method for unscripted documentary. The cutting in this film is almost entirely on colour, hardly ever (if ever) on action. Yes well, maybe on action – or movement – as a movement in itself. So it is in a way very abstract.

But of course all art has that 'abstract' element in it. To make a painting or whatever that is *only* abstract seems to me poco. Just one element of the thing.

So many modern pictures or pieces of sculpture seem like sketches for the real thing or else bits of a whole, fragments equal for instance to the little figure that got broken off and was found among the debris in somebody's garden. Complete in itself, yes, but even more wonderful as part of a greater whole, say a fountain with many figures a church or whatever it was. As the bottles in the Cambio painting were used to decorate a corner of a painting were not the whole painting itself as so often now. (Cristofani)

These films I have been making lately each develop *one* element of film-making (or one chiefly). They are exercises or sketches. – more than sketches. Studies each in one aspect of the technique.

I've probably done enough now of 'assorted views' – assorted shots I mean. Inquadrature assortite. Perugia was like that. Montaggio largely on linear design. The most exploratory thing in LG&K [*The Lion, the Griffin, and the Kangaroo*] was the use of the music and also the use of the words.

In *All These New Relations*[*] I'm exploring to what extent you can join together shots of the same person which have not got continuity of action. It's a thing which gets me when writing scripts. I mean I find *I don't know* sometimes whether there would be a jerk

---

[*]   *All These New Relations* was added to the Scottish Screen Archives collection in 2010. [SN]

if you cut from a person doing something to the same person in different clothes in a different place doing either the same thing or something else. I think you can do it more often than the books say and avoid gongs and 'Ten Years Later' and some continuity devices.

In Mummy's portrait it's that + cutting on colour.

(30 January 1953)

Independence: Small Budget Production in Rome

In Italy there's probably more freedom and independence for cinema directors than there is in most countries. But freedom to make your own films once you have established your name is a different thing from freedom to enter the field in the first place. In an Art in which there is so much big money this is always going to be difficult. But one way in which an able and self-confident but unknown director can get a film to make is by undertaking the production himself, even if it be on a very small scale.

Rome is a *centre* of cinema, that is of cinema as an art even more than of cinema as a speculative enterprise. The people are enthusiastic about the cinema; they love films and the comments one overhears in bars and restaurants are critical and a good deal more adult than the 'Who's in it?' type of discussion I seem to have heard so much of. Intelligent persons discuss cinema as elsewhere they discuss literature or painting. In fact the cinema is taken as seriously as any other art – remembering that serious in Italian does not mean solemn and that the Italians exult in the arts instead of pulling long faces about them.

This status of being a 'centre' is kept up, and subject matter for the discussions is provided by the liveliness of production here. There are always two or three important directors making important films as well as countless minor productions going on. And everybody *knows* about the films in production, – indeed one meets the companies filming in the streets all the year round. There in the Piazza di Spagna was Emmer making his *Le Ragazze della Piazza di Spagna*, while at the top of the stairs Fellini was shooting another film, and at the same time De Sica, taking a rest from directing, was acting in *Buongiorno Elefante* in a suburban street.

All this creates a climate, and it is little wonder that students of the cinema are attracted to Rome not only from all over Italy but from all over the world. As students, they mostly go to the Centro Sperimentale di Cinematografia. This experimental centre of cinema study was founded in 1936 and was a thriving concern before the war. In the war its premises were occupied by successive armies and much of its valuable equipment was stolen. Its excellent archives contained an unusually complete collection of classic films, which was bodily removed to Germany and has not been recovered, and the Centro is with great patience building up a fresh collection. The Centro as a teaching centre has not yet quite succeeded in getting back on its feet after the disintegration it suffered with the war; but the building is there and the equipment is being renewed and is already very adequate; and the students come. So it is a meeting ground for young enthusiasts from Italy, Chile, Argentina, United States, India, Turkey, Egypt, Brazil, Great Britain, – in fact, everywhere. This is perhaps the most important function of the Centro Sperimentale at present.

The Italian student directors are given practice with shooting short scenes in the studios of the Centro along with student cameramen and student actors and actresses, and at the end of their second year they are encouraged to make one short complete film each. Many of them then find employment as assistants in big productions. Others prefer to remain independent and direct their own films even if this means that they can only hope to make shorts and documentaries for many years.

For the foreign students there is no provision for practical work at the Centro, so that if they want to make films they must organise their own practical experience. A group of two or three may get together and finance a short film out of their own pockets or scholarships. This at any rate is what happened last year. Fernando Birri, Peter Hollander and I decided to work together to make a film at our own expense. Peter Hollander got hold of a second-hand Paillard-Bolex 16mm camera and taught himself to operate it. I wrote a detailed shooting script for a simple story to take place entirely in exteriors in Rome. There were two acting parts. Carmen Papio, a young Italian girl who had never acted before, played the lead, and the other part was played by Sergio Rusconi, a student actor at the Centro Sperimentale.

Peter Hollander was a commercial artist in New York before coming to Italy to study cinema so he had already a thorough understanding of design, and camera work came naturally to him.

Fernando Birri, who on that film was an assistant director, is a young Argentine poet, already well known in South America for his poetry and for his stage productions and marionette theatre. The result of this piece of international co-operation was *One is One*, a 30-minute fugue-like silent film which we shot in three weeks and completed in about two months. We like it but we look on it now chiefly as an exercise.

Since then Fernando Birri has directed, for Sperimentalfilm, *Selinunte, i tempi Coricati* a documentary about the astonishing Greek remains at Selinunte, in Sicily. Sperimentalfilm is a co-operative society of people under thirty who produce films because they like them and not hoping for any great financial gain. They aim to make documentaries of cultural value, and educational films. The society was founded in 1951 by Alfonso and Agostino Sansone of Palermo, and many of its members are students of Centro Sperimentale.

Others who work more or less on their own are Leonard Heilige and Henry Croschicki who have made a number of documentaries together, notably *City Without Wheels* an interesting colour film about Venice, using the Cristiani-Mascarini Additcolor Process, Dick Bagley (cameraman of *The Quiet One*), who has made a documentary about the island Ponza, and Dino Partesano whose *Vivo di Te* won a prize at the Venice festival last year. Partesano is at present at work on a short story-film *Angela Non Rubare!* in which Fernando Birri acts the part of a policeman.

Peter Hollander and I have just finished *The Lion, the Griffin, and the Kangaroo*, a documentary about Perugia and the University for Foreigners there. This was sponsored partly by the University for Foreigners and partly by the United States Information Service and the American Commission for Cultural Exchange with Italy. We were fortunate in being allowed considerable freedom by our imaginative sponsors, who realized that a film has to reflect the point of view of those who are actually making it and that for their own, propaganda, purposes a film which is a coherent work of art is more useful than a hotch-potch of what everyone thinks ought to be in it. Ulysses Kay (composer for *The Quiet One*) wrote the music and directed the recording of it, and the rest of it was done entirely by ourselves – preparation of the script, direction and camera work (with our own cameras), cutting and editing, writing and speaking the commentary; we even acted small parts sometimes when there was nobody else to hand.

This film was made on 16 mm, partly for economical reasons

and partly because 16mm is more useful for the sort of distribution the film is to have. But in Italy in general there is a certain contempt for 16mm which is hard to explain. It is not yet looked on as the tool of the experimentalist which it is considered to be in the United States and Great Britain. The consequence is that laboratories are not well equipped for 16mm work and processing is often slipshod. (As a matter of fact, considering the vitality of the Italian film industry and the imaginativeness and general high level of Italian films, the standard of photography and laboratory work in general, and not only in 16mm, is appallingly low.) 16 mm does however offer a freedom and a close contact with the medium which is not always so easy to get in 35 mm work. We certainly feel that our experience with 16 mm has been invaluable, but plan to work in 35 mm as soon as possible.

We are now looking for other producers. Fernando Birri is planning another documentary for Sperimentalfilm, Heilige and Croschicki are always busy, and Partesano is cutting his *Angela, Non Rubare!* And these are not the only people working enthusiastically and independently for next to no money in Rome. The whole place is a hive of this sort of activity.

(to Gavin Lambert, British Film Institute, 27 February 1952)

On Throwing a Film Festival

Festivals, in the sense in which the word is used in this century, are all advertisements of something or other, – of the place where they take place, of the products of exhibitors, performers and decorators. The Edinburgh International Festival of Music and Drama is a tourist draw for Edinburgh, and for performers a showground for their talent. This ready-made showground is utilised by the Edinburgh Film Festival and by numerous independent theatrical companies who have works to present to the receptive public, – because the one thing that is exceptional about the Edinburgh Festival is the public. The operas, the plays, the musical pieces performed might occur in any average week in London or New York. Not so the public. For the city is crammed full for three weeks with people who have come from far away with just one idea of seeing as many shows as possible. And for those three weeks in the year all the citizens of Edinburgh too become art-lovers, opera-mad, crazy about theatre, music and film.

I had films to show, produced by myself and the two groups I work with, Ancona Films and Sperimental Film, and a place to show them in, in Edinburgh, so I decided to use this festival time of public receptivity to show our wares. In my workrooms in Rose Street, Edinburgh I fitted out a small theatre. The biggest room has a reasonable length of throw for the projector and very nice acoustics for sound reproduction. A couple of small windows daringly made in an intervening wall turned a neighbouring small room into a projection booth. Ingenious if slightly confusing manipulation of switches and leads by a colleague gave me adequate control of theatre lights etc. from a central point. My New York partner, Peter Hollander, designed us an excellent poster, I had invitation cards printed, and advertised as well as I could the coming 'Rose Street Film Festival'.

I checked with the Police that there was no objection to my holding such a show provided I didn't charge for admission. At the last minute the rain started coming through the roof of our condemned premises, but even that was righted after one uncomplaining audience had got a minor wetting.

The shows were at 7 p.m. and at 11 p.m. each evening. 11 p.m. was for people who had been to some other show in town but weren't yet ready to call it a day, and it proved to be popular.

As people came up our narrow stairs they usually wondered, 'Is this the right place?' When they were asked into our reception room and given a cup of coffee they wondered all the more. Sometimes when there were not very many in the audience they looked very doubtful indeed. – *Have* we come to the right place? But those doubtful faces underwent a remarkable and gratifying change of expression during the performance, and when I met the visitors in the theatre after the show they were usually very happy to stay on awhile and talk about films and other things and drink Italian coffee.

The programme was as follows.

ALFABETO NOTTURNO, made by Agostino and Alfonso Sansone, Fernando Birri and Peter Hollander in Sicily in 1952, an account of evening school in the tiny mountain village of Torretta in the heart of Giuliana country.

THE LION, THE GRIFFIN, AND THE KANGAROO, made by Peter Hollander and Margaret Tait in 1951–52, a film sponsored by the city of Perugia and the Italian University for Foreigners, by U.S.I.S.

[United States Information Service] and the Fulbright Commission, about the mediaeval and once warlike city which now is a meeting place for foreign students.

SELINUNTE, THE FALLEN TEMPLES, made by Fernando Birri in 1951, a study of the Greek ruins at Selinunte in southern Sicily.

DIMITRI WORKS IN BLACK WAX, made by Peter Hollander in Rome in 1952, an account of the lost wax method of casting and a study of the sculptor, Dimitri Hadzi.

A PORTRAIT OF GA, a colour portrait of an old lady, made by Margaret Tait in 1952–53.

Projection was all on 16mm, and in fact all of the films except *Selinunte* were produced on 16mm. Since 1952 Sperimentalfilm have produced *Centrale Termo-Elettrica* and *Immagini Popolari Siciliane* but were unable to send 16mm copies of those. In the second week of the festival I received from New York Ancona Films' two most recent productions, SOMETIMES A NEWSPAPER, made by Peter Hollander in 1953–54 and SHAPES, a colour film for children made by Peter Hollander, Miriam Schlein and Hermann Gottesmann in 1954.

We aim to make films neither for the specialist nor for the hypothetical moronic 'mass' but for the intelligent general public. Personally I disagree with all attempts to 'raise the level of public taste'. I think we have our work cut out satisfying the demand for entertainment at a high level that already exists. Since our films are mostly on 16mm they usually get shown to specialised audiences, and I had had no opportunity of judging their impact on a general audience.

Rose Street is known as rather a tough street, and I was afraid our films would not appeal to the local inhabitants, and rather hoped they wouldn't come up. After the festival had been going on for about a week they suddenly noticed it and I had a visit first of all from three or four small children from the street who sat quietly through the performance and declared that they had enjoyed it. Then the Rose Street children began to accost me daily in the street with 'Is there films tonight, missis?' and for a day or two gangs of them came to the seven o'clock performance. But they got a bit noisy and disturbed the rest of the audience, so I had to keep the children out of the evening shows, promising them a show for themselves later on. The first time that I was saying at the street door, 'No, I'm sorry, no children in the evenings' a couple of teenage boys who habitually stand in the doorway opposite dressed in the current 'teddy-boy' fashion (popularly and rather ingenuously supposed to be favoured by delinquents only) strode across and entered, to show the children how grownup *they* were I suppose. At that performance, as luck would have it, an amplifier valve blew, but the boys didn't want to leave. I guess they preferred not to face the children in the street, who would no doubt infer that they had been turned out, so I showed them the whole programme silent. They came back the next evening and saw it again, with sound. They returned a third evening with two other young boys. There were other people too who came to see the films several times, and I made some new friends this way.

Many people came to the Rose Street Festival after a concert in the Usher Hall or after the opera, and they certainly added a festival 'atmosphere'. Some of the most appreciative members of our audiences were practising artists in other fields – architects, musicians, a few painters, one poet. It was very encouraging for me to get so much appreciation from the very people I would *like* to like the films, – direct people, genuine people, and it was a great joy that most of my visitors were like that. There were only very few who had the upside-down sophisticated state of mind which I associate with a certain type of suburban film society member, hack reporters, and the sort of smart alec who must always be in the know and in the fashion. Those upside-down people were the only ones who didn't care for our films. They said they were 'hoping for something more experimental' or 'WHY did I make these films?' as if they couldn't understand anyone going to any trouble to make a film that is quite lucid. Those people puzzle me because they all *know* about films, they probably *can* reel off a list of all Chaplin's films and *do* appreciate the recognised classics and enjoy anything securely labelled 'experimental' (and therefore probably already some years out of date as an experiment), and I dare say their opinion is of some sort of importance in a way. But it is not important to me in my work, and I don't want to make films for them because the things they want always seem to me in some way phoney. It is as if they had difficulty in understanding anything straightforward and clear.

Ancona Films and Sperimentalfilm productions are straightforward. Most of them do contain experimental work, but just some experiment of our own. Each of our films has been made about a subject we consider interesting in itself, and it was very nice that in the discussions which our audiences carried on it was the subject of the film that they discussed rather than the film as film.

The technique of the lost wax method of casting was entered into, the direct method of language teaching, the problem of illiteracy in remote Sicilian villages, the nature of the stone in Selinunte and Perugia, and so on. Audiences were small and so the talk was very direct and informal.

I was particularly pleased by the response of Edinburgh people. I found a very keen positive interest in films and enthusiasm for the idea of more films being produced in Scotland, especially by Scottish independents. Of course there must always have been a positive feeling for film in Edinburgh for the Film Guild to have been formed in the first place and to have grown into the Edinburgh Film Festival. This latter has become very much of a 'festival proper'. Rose Street as a street has a reputation for being improper, and although the Rose Street Film Festival is in no danger of becoming improper, I intend to keep it unofficial and individual.

(December 1954)

Close-up of Rose Street

It's noisy all the time. Lorries rattle by or wait throbbing with anger for the jam to clear. Great whalebacks of furniture vans pass at first-floor window level. Bottles jabber against each other, full thuddy ones going into the voracious pubs, empty ones in cases emptily being returned or in crazy assortment arriving at Mr Gibb's empty-bottle shop for classification and disposal.

The shop was once a school. The floor slopes downwards to the back. Where the overlooking desks once were are crates and garlands, of whisky bottles, wine bottles, ketchup bottles. Shelves hold miniature bottles and gigantic display bottles. In the window a treat of brown and green glass. A shaft of sunlight from the back window lights a beam of dust and turns plain undressed wood into the most exotic material on earth. A curved doorway leads into mysterious quarters beyond. An old fancy weighing machine and a new fancy arrangement for ringing a bell are so individual that they seem magic.

Across the way, Mr Lumsden in his doorway touches his hat to a passing duke and leers for fun at the girl from the sweetie counter. Tap tap tap of high heels makes him turn his head this way and that way. Mr Lumsden is very polite. Mr Lumsden watches everything. Mr Lumsden's shop is a jumble of cast-off tit-bits in alluring disarray.

'Chips, my dear?' says Joe. The wee boys are chased out of the café because they disturb the other customers. 'Film stars have been here. All sorts of people have drunk coffee at my tables.' Joe is a film star himself. Well, he appears in a short film called *Rose Street*.

John Burns ran across the street and got chips at Joe's. John's bright little face has the typical liveliness of the children who live in Rose Street. With Philip and Douglas and George and Harry and Billy and a crowd of others he takes possession – the children take possession when the traffic is gone and the shops are closed. Church bells don't worry them. They play peever [hopscotch] on the pavement and build the dust in the gutter into shapes for their games.

'I'm no speakan to you,' said Frances Rosie loftily, seated on the kerb, her face all covered with the black off her hands which had been scraping up happy heaps of sooty debris. 'Have you got a car? – Well, I don't like you, then.'

The girls skip, and play with balls and bicycles, and jump out the peever formula. The boys play football and cowboys, some-times peever with the girls, and bicycle the circle round the Rose Street Lane and back; and boys and girls together have wild wonderful fun playing chainy tig in the back lane. Girls are the ones who know the singing games, the beautiful, the fantastic, the traditional, the profound. Old lore makes lassies' games. Boys follow the radio and comics more.

Suddenly they grow up and stand in doorways. They smoke and take an interest in their clothes. 'You're just teddy boys,' the children chanted at them one day. But they're not, for they retain the Rose Street centre-of-the-world openness. Well, – they have adolescent exaggerated enthusiasms. Girls buy two, perhaps three, records, and the whole street rocks and trembles to full-volume rock 'n' roll repetition of the same tunes every Sunday from breakfast to bedtime and at intervals in the week.

Unsavoury Rose Street – what a laugh! Just mention the name of the street, and Edinburgh folk either laugh or tut-tut with disap-proval. 'An article about Rose Street?' they say, their eyes bursting. 'It wouldn't be printable.'

In Rose Street there are fourteen pubs, – Miss Scott's, Forrest's, the Gordon Arms, the Rose and Crown, the Kenilworth, Scarlett's, the Auld Hundred, the White Cockade, Paddy Crossan's, Wm. Nicol's Bar, the Canmore Vaults, the Bon-Accord, Crane's Bar, the Abbotsford. When we were filming the interior of a pub for the short film, *Rose Street,* we planned the shooting for a Saturday evening, at a time it was likely to be full. We asked the proprietress to confirm our views on this. 'Well, it depends on whether Hearts win,' she said. But Friday night is drinking night really, and is the only evening that the street is as noisy as in the daytime, as a rule, – except, of course, for the time that Hearts won the *Cup.*

In Rose Street there is a police box, from which pairs of policemen go out at regular intervals and carefully pace the length of the street. The children at their games threaten each other with, 'Here comes a bobby.' The bobby's chief preoccupation by daytime is to keep the traffic from getting stuck, by politely moving on waiting vehicles, and in the night to see that shops and stores are secure.

I never counted the prostitutes. I am sorry to be so ignorant but I don't really know if there are more in Rose Street than elsewhere. It must be the presence of the pubs which gives Rose Street a vague reputation for unspecified vice. Or could it be the bleak red office buildings – Menzies Ltd., the Telephone Exchange, the Labour Exchange, Stewarts' printing works, with blind eyes to the street and the lane and one great heavy doorway each, gushing forth little imported factory girls for lunch hours and the eleven o'clock pieces? Those blank products of the Industrial age have a more vicious frown than the jolly pubs, more vicious than the simply beautiful and beautifully simple domestic buildings which line the street in varied similarity. In those teeming houses and up those busy stairs live people.

But nevertheless it has that reputation. There must be something in it, you'd think. This boisterous healthy street, named after the English rose, built in the eighteenth century to house the tradesmen who then kept small shops to supply the fine folk of brand-new Princes Street and George Street, a narrow street where now the sparrows can be heard twittering, even shouting, in the eaves above the yell of the traffic, where the seagull calls through the echo of St Cuthbert's bells, and the distant screech of a train whistle is not really very far away at all, only across two rows of buildings, in the valley of Princes Street Gardens (one of the play-grounds of the children here), where the bairns and the housewife can see from the back-kitchen window the floodlit gaunt castle while father is watching racing on television in the parlour, has for a reason it might well be fun to discover that laughter-provoking unsavoury connotation.

'It could be made a second Bond Street,' say the hat-shop ladies, wishfully.

'It could be made a second Soho,' say restaurant proprietors.

'Something could be done about it. It could be a second something else from somewhere else.'

But it won't be. It will stay the first and only Rose Street, Edinburgh.

'We ought to develop it, ' say the planners. 'Pull it all down and use it for a bottle-neck car-park.'

'No, no, no. Pull it all down and build some nice gloomy offices.'

'No, no. Just pull it down.'

'Why pull down the humbly elegant buildings? The bumptious grim ones are less worth leaving.'

'Ah, I see you're just a traditionalist. Hehehe.'

'Vicious Rose Street! Ha ha ha!'

Published in *Scotland's Magazine*, 53, 12 December 1957

Two-way Drift

Too many people leave the country and move into the towns. Too many people leave the islands and move to the mainland. It is called a 'drift', and so it is like a drift, as if a great elemental force were carrying with it individual particles that perhaps didn't particularly mean to go in that direction.

How many is too many is a matter of opinion. There *is* a very general feeling that too many drift, although those that express the opinion may then join the drift into the towns.

On the other hand, some go back. And perhaps it is a process that has been going on for longer than we realise – a drift of people away from one place into another, and then maybe a drift back again of different people from the overcrowded places out into the fertile spaces.

In Orkney, the drift is in two stages. Families from the smaller islands drift to the Mainland of Orkney, and people from the Orkney Mainland go away to the Scottish mainland, or to Canada and other places.

Last winter, I made a short film in the form of a news magazine, for the Orkney Education Committee, about two families who had decided to drift *back* to Orkney. George Tait and his family returned to Ingsay in Birsay after some years of farming in Aberdeenshire. Neil Flaws went to Habreck in the island of Wyre. Habreck is where he was born, but he trained as a blacksmith and worked in the naval base of Lyness and then went away to Halifax in Yorkshire, where he had a good job with a firm of welders. His Irish wife, Alice, was a nurse in Halifax. Their two children, John and Sheila, are Yorkshire-born.

A brother of Neil's and a cousin, have farms in Wyre too. There are eight farms in the island – all now occupied – and a population of thirty-eight, seven children at school, and four younger children not yet at school.

It is the island where Edwin Muir spent his early childhood – at the farm of the Bu, close to Cubbie Roo's Castle, and in his Autobiography he gives a warm picture of Wyre. It *is* a warm island, well worth drifting back to. The farmers of Wyre are active and prosperous. The island is fertile, and rewarding to farm. They have difficulties of their own, the chief of which is transport. Men are all right in small boats, and so are children, but some of the women would rather be able to step onto a steamer from a pier when they go into town. But on Wyre there is no pier, only a jetty for small boats.

The lack of a pier is almost the only thing the Wyre people complain about. One was to be built, and then the 'credit squeeze' stopped it. It's a business loading farm produce from a small jetty on to small boats and then transferring it all to the steamer lying outby, particularly when there are cattle, sheep and pigs to go. They have a big coal cobble now for this sort of thing, and even tractors have come ashore in it. (Every farm in Wyre has at least one tractor, but there are no cars to go along the few miles of public highway.)

Nobody who doesn't live on an island can quite realise how important is a pier.

Before the last war there was a daily air service carrying mail and passengers to the North Isles of Orkney, but wartime restrictions stopped it; and then, with the air services becoming nationalised, somehow it has never been possible to resume those services to individual islands which the private companies used to run. There have been several attempts to start a privately run service again, but they have failed to get enough support.

That, in fact, is one of the reasons why people drift away from the isles. Why they or others drift back again is because they love the place.

Colour Poems 1974

I was trying to get an impression, from the back of my mind, of some news photographs (mostly in *Picture Post*) and newsreel shots of thirty-seven – thirty-eight years earlier in one bitter winter of the Spanish Civil War of men stuck up in trees, with rifles, and apparently frozen, some of them had been shot and were slumped over a branch and then frozen there by the severe weather and (a memory which may not be a true one) some of them had even frozen to death, tucked in a notch of the branches of a tree. It was such a pathetic, heartbreaking image [...] I had an image in my mind, but a shaky image, a composite of what I remembered and what I thought I remembered and some feeling remaining from that time of the immense sorrow of it (of men being pushed to such extremes) and the tragic poetic thing about the Spanish Civil War which is what seems to have come down from that time.

The unsteadiness and the persistence of such images as I had is what I tried to convey in these sketches on the emulsion of the film. The scratching out of them was not consciously at the time to do with the 'etched on the memory' kind of idea (I don't think so). I scratched them out, frame by frame – actually one frame in three, leaving two blank trying to repeat the same drawing each time, but not of course achieving an identical picture – so it's the opposite of 'nude descending a staircase' where a painter might try to repre-sent a succession of moments all in one canvas, I was repeating the same drawing over several moments. A free drawing each time, to some guidelines to keep it from flickering about the screen *too* much (but needing the inevitable flicker to convey the instabilitiy and the persistence both at the same time. [...]

I wasn't trying to 'animate' it with progressive movement from frame to frame, I was trying to keep it the same – there were bound to be slight differences and I counted on these differences to give a sort of *shiver* to the image on the screen which was meant to be like the shivering of the image I was trying to catch in my own memory – at the back of my mind. I had been reading Sorley MacLean, *Poems to Eimhir* in which the poet seems heartbroken about his own failure to go and fight in Spain *choosing* instead to spend the summer with the girl he was in love with. This made me try to recall what I could about those times, before the war and what came to mind were those photographs. The title 'Numen of the Boughs' came from a phrase in Lorca's 'Poet in New York' and there suddenly was the image to illustrate that with – that phrase – men of the branches.

(1982)

Colour Poems 1974

Well, yes
I do remember
the young men
going off to fight in Spain
but not Sorley MacLean.
not Sorley MacLean in his pain –

then them coming back, changed,
and yet not changed enough
for my notion then,
of what war might be.

frozen soldiers of the plains,
stiff in trees,
in photographs
the black showing through the thin snow
on the hard plain of Madrid
as shown to us in newsreels
stick in my vision
and click now with Maclean's poem 'to Eimhir'
and Lorca's *Numen of the Boughs*
busy with studies then
and enjoying ourselves,
How much did we notice?

I remember the look of young men
Coming back
who had been in Spain
And wondering about them

what took them there?
what brought them back?
What had they learned?
what sad knowledge was for evermore
buried deep inside them?

Film-poem or Poem-film: A few notes about film and poetry from Margaret Tait

In my self-made films I'm always looking at where I am at the time, considering at length my immediate surroundings and 'making use of available actuality' as I used to say. But in the feature scripts, which are fictional, imaginary situations are what I use. (Only one of those screenplays, BLUE BLACK PERMANENT, has so far been realised on film.) Surroundings, in making a fiction film, whether all sets built specifically for the film or partly 'real', i.e. real places standing in for imaginary places, and props made for the part or at least sought out, chosen and placed, or maybe just 'found' already there, can end up being used in much the same way, – I mean, stared at, brought into the imaginary whole along with their own actuality.

The contradictory or paradoxical thing is that in a *Documentary* the real things depicted are liable to lose their reality by being photographed and presented in that 'documentary' way, and there's no poetry in that. In poetry, something else happens. Hard to say what it is. Presence, let's say, soul or spirit, an empathy with whatever it is that's dwelt upon, felling for it, to the point of iden-tification.

On the other hand, I have at times been imbued with the idea of making a film to illustrate or to 'set' (in the sense of *setting* a poem to music) an existing poem, a known poem, and an early effort of mine was to set Hopkins' 'The Leaden Echo and the Golden Echo' to pictures. In HUGH MACDIARMID, A PORTRAIT I did something similar, by *setting* my picture to 'Somersault' and 'Krang' as spoken by MacDiarmid. Different from 'The Eemis Stane' which is in the film with its musical setting, as a totality, and the picture during that is 'incidental'. Then again, the third poem that MacDiarmid reads, 'You Know Not Who I Am', which opens the film and closes it, is used by me more as a comment on the film as a whole and on the partiality to be expected of a PORTRAIT.

I think that film is essentially a poetic medium, and although it can be put to all sorts of other – creditable and discreditable – uses, these are secondary.

The great joy of directing BLUE BLACK PERMANENT was in working with the cast and the crew, each bringing their own qualities into the feeling of the whole thing.

It's mainly the actors and actresses who give so much greater scope in a feature compared to a short. They and the characters they create bring it into quite a different dimension from what one can do working away by oneself with a camera and an editing bench. Even all the organisation associated with having performers affects the dimension. One of the miracles about film is that that, and all the complications of production on a wider scale, don't have to quell the poetry that's inherent in what's being made, so long as it is there in the first place.

Published in Peter Todd (ed.), *Poem Film Film Poem*, 2, November 1997

Video Poems for the 90s (working title)

With Celtic art – Celtic culture very much in mind i.e. (inc.) the end in the beginning, the beginning in the end (e.g. intertwined serpents with the head swallowing the tail) in so much of Celtic design – jewellery, book illumination, crosses, stonework…

Animated title using this design idea – then nine themes, interlocking:

1 A child reading – a simple image, contemplating the intent way in which a young child reads, or looks at a book, meeting the world of storybook or picture book. Hold it – Hold it simple – Hold it direct.
2 The edge of the sea. Literally the very edge where shore meets water – life on both sides. [Here Margaret Tait has a little drawing of edge of the sea, a symbol, but also a reality. P.T and B.C.]
3 Birds in wilderness – ('Here we sit like birds in the wilderness') Real birds – Real wilderness. ('In and out the dusty bluebells') (Melancholic bird calls) (Bees)
4 Stock on the Road. Touch of incongruity, touch of 'what are they

doing there?' whiff of ineffable sadness (if not tragedy) in the fate of all creatures – Insistence through several instances of stock-moving, stock straying or finding its way out – or being driven along willy-nilly –

5 Rust everywhere. Plenty of instances of this. Rather inanimate, rather static, but, nevertheless, implied in the crumbling machinery the dwindled fencing and gateposts is that nothing stays the same.

6 Heavy Traffic – Oh yes! Far from rusted yet. The maintained, the oiled, the useful, the busy.

7 Flight to and from – comes out of six – articulated lorries entering the ferry, heavy car doors, the leaving and arriving – Aircraft, different sizes, up and away, down and in – Sailboats and other boats – A busy scene – Where do they all come from? Where are they all going? The birds too, they flock and wheel and prepare to leave. Flight of individual birds.

8 Crash of a wave – a direct statement – An irrefutable image –

9 Turning a page. The quiet page turning by the grown person – (with echoes perhaps of a device in many film titles).

Then animated decoration again in the titles.

Published in Peter Todd and Ben Cook (eds.)
Subjects and Sequences: A Margaret Tait Reader (2004)

RESOURCES

Works by Margaret Tait

Books

The Grassy Stories: Short Stories for Children (Edinburgh: M.C. Tait, 1959)
Lane Furniture: A Book of Stories (Edinburgh: M.C. Tait, 1959)
origins and elements, poems (Edinburgh: M.C. Tait, 1959). Cover by Peter Hollander
The Hen and the Bees: Legends and Lyrics, poems (Edinburgh: M.C. Tait, 1960). Cover by Robin Philipson
Subjects and Sequences, poems (Edinburgh: M.C. Tait, 1960)

Essays

'Close-up of Rose St', *Scotland's Magazine*, December 1957, vol. 53, no. 12, pp. 8–11
'Making Films About Scotland' ['Points of View' section], *The Scotsman* (2 February 1957): 7
'The Day I Bathed in the Roman Baths', *Edinburgh Evening News*, Monday 6 November 1961, p. 3
'Films by Margaret Tait', statement, *Time Out*, no. 22, 18 April 1980, p. 45. Reprinted in *Poem Film Film Poem*, no. 5, December 1999, pp 1–3
'Orkney Film Maker on Tour', *The Orcadian*, Thursday 19 May 1988, p. 7
Statement on six films selected by filmmaker as 'models for a representation of Scotland on screen', in Kenny Mathieson (ed.), *Desperately Seeking Cinema?*, Glasgow Film Theatre, May–October 1988, pp. 83–4
'George Mackay Brown Remembered', *Chapman*, no. 84, 1996, pp. 33–4
'A Few Notes about Film and Poetry', in Peter Todd (ed.) *Poem Film Film Poem*, no. 2, November 1997, pp 4–5
'Garden Pieces, Their Slow Evolution', in Peter Todd (ed.), *Poem Film Film Poem*, no. 5, December 1999, pp 1–3

Selected Bibliography

'The Drift Back', review, *Film User*, vol. 11, no. 130, August 1957, p. 340
'Experimental Film in the Orkneys', *Today's Cinema*, vol. 88, no. 7765, 30 April 1957, p. 4
'Feature: New Scottish Filmmakers', Margaret Tait in her own words, *The List*, 10–23 April 1992
'Festival Notes: Film Portrait', *The Scotsman*, 31 August 1954, p. 6
'Film Experiment in Orkney: "The Drift Back"', *The Scotsman*, 15 April 1957, p. 8
'Mags, 73, in Blue Movie!', *The Scottish Sun*, 4 June 1992
'Margaret Tait', obituary, *The Times*, 28 May 1999, p. 31
'Orcadian's Film for Edinburgh Festival?', *The Orkney Herald*, 25 July 1957, p. 4

'Orkney Magazine Film', *The Orkney Herald*, 8 January 1957, p. 2

'Perugia Film Real Triumph for Students', *The Daily American*, Travel Supplement, 31 March 1952

'*Portrait of Ga*', review, *Film User*, vol. 9, no. 100, January 1955, p. 108

'Three Jubilee Film Shows', *The Orcadian*, 22 September 1977

A.B., 'Celluloid Experiment', *The Scotsman*, August 1954

Ute Aurand, 'Margaret Tait', Margaret Tait Film Tour programme brochure (Berlin: Ute Aurand, 1994)

Ute Aurand, 'Die Filmpoetin Margaret Tait ist gestorben', *Film*, no. 6, 1999, pp. 4–5

Gavin Bell, 'A Reel Visionary', *The Scotsman*, 27 September 2000, p. 14

David Bruce, 'Rose Street: Margaret Tait and Women in Scottish Film', *Scotland: The Movie* (London: Polygon, 1996), pp. 108–9

Noel Burch, 'Narrative/Diegesis-Thresholds, limits', *Screen*, vol. 23, no. 2, July–August 1982, pp. 16–33

George Clark, 'Aspects of Change: The Fifty-Eighth Edinburgh International Film Festival', *Senses of the Cinema*, no. 33, October–December 2004, www.sensesofcinema.com/2004/festivals-reports/edinburgh2004

Adrienne Cochrane, 'If You Really Look', review of Margaret Tait's *Selected Films 1952–1976*, *PN Review* 174, vol. 33, no. 4, March–April 2007

Beatrice Colin, 'Tidemarks', *The List*, 23 April–6 May 1993, p. 27

Jo Comino, 'Place of Work', *Monthly Film Bulletin*, 1983

Benjamin Cook and Peter Todd, 'Margaret Tait', National Film Theatre programme booklet, October 2000, pp. 34–5

Torcuil Crichton, 'Film Honour for Orkney's Movie Poet', *The Sunday Herald* (Glasgow), 17 September 2000, p. 10

Laura Cumming, 'Poetry in Motion Pictures', *The Observer*, 'Review', 8 November 2009, p. 14

David Curtis, 'Britain's Oldest Experimentalist... Margaret Tait', *Vertigo*, no. 9, Summer 1999, pp. 62–3

——, 'In Her Own Words', in Peter Todd and Benjamin Cook (eds.) *Subjects and Sequences: A Margaret Tait Reader* (London: LUX, 2004), pp. 77–98

Barry Didcock, 'Setting the Art World Alight', *The Sunday Herald*, 'The Arts', 11 October 2009, pp. 4–7

Ninian Dunnett, 'New Director Makes Feature Debut at Age of 73', *The Sunday Times*, Scotland, Arts, 3 May 1992, p. 4

Derek Elley, '*Blue Black Permanent*', review, *Variety*, 14 December 1992

Gareth Evans, 'Only Connect: The Secret Art of Film Poems', *Filmwaves*, Autumn 1999, pp. 28–30

——, 'Where I Am is Here: A Patchwork for Margaret Tait', in Peter Todd and Benjamin Cook (eds.) *Subjects and Sequences: A Margaret Tait Reader* (London: LUX, 2004), pp. 35–50

Elizabeth Ewan, Sue Innes, Sian Reynolds, Rose Pipes (eds.), *The*

Biographical Dictionary of Scottish Women (Edinburgh: Edinburgh University Press, 2007)

Monika Fabig, 'Report about Women Filmmakers in Independent Film: Germaine Dulac, Maya Deren, Margaret Tait', Hamburg, 1987

David Finch, 'Film-Maker as Poet: Films by Stan Brakhage, Bruce Baillie and Margaret Tait', catalogue, European Media Art Festival (1–11 September), Osnabruck, 1988

Lizzie Francke, 'Sea Song', *Every Woman*, April 1993, p. 23

Philip French, 'Ripening Parable of Perfection', *The Observer*, 4 April 1993, p. 54

Chris Garratt, 'Margaret Tait's Films', catalogue, the Celtic Mirror Festival, Falmouth, Kernow, 10–12 November, 1989, p. 4

Ian Goode, 'Scottish Cinema and Scottish Imaginings: *Blue Black Permanent* and *Stella Does Tricks*', *Screen*, vol. 46, no. 2, Summer 2005, pp. 235–9

Kevin Gough-Yates, 'Moving Pictures', *Art Monthly*, June 1983, p. 33

Yvonne Gray, 'Margaret Tait, Orkney Poet and Film-Maker Remembered', review of Peter Todd and Benjamin Cook (eds.), *Subjects and Sequences: A Margaret Tait Reader* (London: LUX, 2004), *Northwords Now*, 2007

Murray Grigor, 'Margaret Tait', obituary, *The Independent*, 12 May 1999, p. 6

——, Twenty-Fourth Edinburgh Film Festival brochure, 1970, pp. 52–4, reprinted in Peter Todd and Benjamin Cook (eds.), *Subjects and Sequences: A Margaret Tait Reader* (London: LUX, 2004), p. 141

Wally Hammond, '*Blue Black Permanent*: NFT', *Time Out*, 31 March – 7 April 1993, p. 53

——, '*Blue Black Permanent*', review, *Time Out*, 31 March – 7 April 1993, p. 6

Donna Heddle, '*Subjects and Sequences*': *A Margaret Tait Reader*, review, *Scottish Studies Review*, 2006, pp. 110–11

Nan Heriot, 'Rose Street Comes to Life – for 20 Minutes', *The Bulletin*, 10 July 1957, p. 10

Allan Hunter, '*Blue Black Permanent*', *Screen International*, no. 862, 19 June 1992, pp. 20–21

Jeremy Isaacs, *Storm Over 4: A Personal Account* (London: Weidenfield & Nicholson, 1989), p.173

Kevin Jackson, 'The Early Promise of Late Starters', *The Independent*, Arts, 17 August 1992, p. 10

Sheila Johnston, '*Blue Black Permanent*', review, *Independent*, 2 April 1993, p. 16

Tamara Kirkorian, 'Margaret Tait', in David Curtis (ed.), *A Directory of British Film and Video Artists* (Luton: University of Luton and The Arts Council of England, 1996), pp. 190–1

——, '*On the Mountain* and *Land Makar*: Landscape and Townscape in Margaret Tait's Work', in Michael Maziere and Nina Danino (eds.), *The 'Undercut' Reader: Critical Writings on Artists' Film and Video* (London:

Wallflower, 2002), pp. 103–5.

Mike Leggett, 'The Autonomous Film-Maker: Margaret Tait: Films and Poems: A Correspondence between Mike Leggett and Margaret Tait', ed. Richard Kwietniowsksi, 1979, British Artists' Film and Video Study Collection, Central Saint Martins College of Art and Design

——, 'Margaret Tait', in David Curtis (ed.), *A Directory of British Film & Video Artists* (Luton: John Libby Media/London: Arts Council of England, 1996), pp. 190–2

——, *'On the Mountain'*, review, *Time Out*, no. 522, 18 April 1980, p. 45

Malcolm Le Grice, 'First Festival of Independent British Cinema', *Studio International*, vol. 189, no. 975, May–June 1975, p. 225

——, Programme notes, Film London: Third Avant-Garde International Festival. London: National Film Theatre, 1979

Hugh MacDiarmid, 'Intimate Film Making in Scotland: The Work of Dr Margaret Tait', *Scottish Field*, October 1960, reprinted in Angus Calder, Glen Murray and Alan Riach (eds.), *The Raucle Tongue* (Manchester: Carcanet, 1998), vol. 3, pp. 415–17

Aonghas Macneacail, 'primula scotia at yesnaby' (for Margaret Tait: 1918–1999), poem, *The Orcadian*, 17 May 1999

Janet McBain and Alan Russell, 'Preserving the Margaret Tait Film Collection', in Peter Todd and Benjamin Cook (eds.), *Subjects and Sequences: A Margaret Tait Reader* (London: LUX, 2004), pp. 101–9

Tony McKibbin, 'The Passing Present', *Anon Five*, 2007, pp. 65–77

——, 'Scottish Cinema: A Victim Culture?', *Cencrastus*, no. 73, 2002, pp. 25–9

Derek Malcolm, *'Blue Black Permanent'*, review, *The Guardian*, 1 April 1993, p. 5

Howard Maxford, 'Blue Black Permanent', review, *What's On In London*, 7 April 1993, p. 35

Rod Mengham, 'Review: Margaret Tait', *Art Monthly* no. 310, October, 2007, p. 39

Mitch Miller, '"…quite unique": Reviving Margaret Tait, In Conversation with Peter Todd', *The Drouth*, Spring 2005, www.thedrouth.org/storage/The%20Drouth%2015-1.pdf

——, 'Re: Margaret Tait: Reverberation, Recognition, Rediscovery', *The Drouth*, Spring 2005, www.thedrouth.org/storage/The%20Drouth%2015-1.pdf

——, 'Recycled, Re-imagined and Resurrected: The Return of Margaret Tait', *Roughcuts*, December/January 2006/7, p. 15

Jan Moir, 'First Person Highly Singular', *The Guardian*, 31 March 1993, pp. 8–9

Edwin Morgan, 'Who Will Publish Scottish Poetry', review of *origins and elements*, *New Saltire* 2, November 1961, pp. 51–6

Edward Nairn, 'Stills from Orquil Burn and Happy Bees', poem, Second Rose Street Film Festival leaflet, August 1955

Sarah Neely, 'Contemporary Scottish Cinema', in Neil Blain and David

Hutchison (eds.), *The Media in Scotland* (Edinburgh: Edinburgh University Press, 2008), pp. 151–65

——, '"Ploughing a lonely furrow": Margaret Tait and "Professional" Filmmaking Practices in 1950s Scotland', in Ian Craven (ed.), *Movies on Home Ground: Explorations in Amateur Cinema* (Newcastle: Cambridge Scholars Press, 2010), pp. 301–26

——, 'Stalking the image: Margaret Tait and Intimate Filmmaking Practices', *Screen*, vol. 49, no. 2, Summer 2008, pp. 216–21

Sarah Neely and Alan Riach, 'Demons in the Machine: Cinema and Modernism in Twentieth-Century Scotland', in Jonathan Murray, Fidelma Farley and Rod Stoneman (eds.), *New Scottish Cinema* (Newcastle: Cambridge Scholars Press, 2009), pp. 1–19

P.C., 'Rose Street Film Festival', *The Edinburgh Evening Dispatch*, August 1954

Duncan Petrie, *Screening Scotland* (London: British Film Institute, 2000), pp.164–5, p.168

Alex Pirie, 'Margaret Tait Film Maker 1918–1999: Indications, Influence, Outcomes', *Poem Film Film Poem*, no. 6, 2000, pp. 1–12

Richard Price, 'Margaret Tait: Film-maker and Poet', *PS*, no. 7, 2011, pp. 22–8

Chitra Ramaswamy, 'Tait Gallery Restored', *Scotland on Sunday*, Arts, 12 November 2006

Judith M. Redding and Victoria Brownworth, 'Margaret Tait', in *Film Fatales* (Seattle: Seal Press), pp. 109–11

Alan Riach, 'Tait's MacDiarmid', poem, *Homecoming: New Poems 2001–2009* (Edinburgh: Luath Press, 2009), p. 164

J.L. Reyner, 'Margaret Tait', in 'Edinburgh Excerpts', *Continental Film Review*, November 1970, p. 9

——, 'Margaret Tait', obituary, *The Guardian*, 13 May 1999, p. 22

Lucy Reynolds, 'Colour Poems', *Poem Film Film Poem*, no. 12, September 2003, pp. 6–7, doubled as programme notes for 'Film Poems 4: Messages', a film programme curated by Peter Todd

——, 'Margaret Tait: Marks of Time', in Peter Todd and Benjamin Cook (eds.) *Subjects and Sequences: A Margaret Tait Reader* (London: LUX, 2004), pp. 57–69

Michael Romer, 'Malcolm Lowry's influence on Orcadian filmmaker Margaret Tait', *The Firminist: A Malcolm Lowry Journal*, no. 2, October 2011, pp. 9–16

——, 'Poetry in *Blue Black Permanent*: Three Footnotes to Margaret Tait's Film', *Cencrastus*, no. 82, February 2006, pp. 8–13

George Rosie, 'A Glimpse of Rare Talent', *The Sunday Times*, 22 August 2004

William Russell, '*Blue Black Permanent*', *The Herald*, 24 April 1993

Sukhdev Sandhu, 'Open Connection', review of Peter Todd and Benjamin Cook (eds.) *Subjects and Sequences: A Margaret Tait Reader* (London: LUX, 2004), *New Statesman*, 7 February 2005, www.newstatesman.com/200502070046

Resources   175

——, 'Unique Vision of a Film Poet', *The Daily Telegraph*, 23 August 2004, p. 17

Ryan Shand, 'A Review of *Subjects and Sequences: A Margaret Tait Reader*', *The Moving Image: The Journal of the Association of Moving Image Archivists*, vol. 7, no. 1, 2007, pp. 107–10

Robert Shure, 'The Long Light Days of Margaret Tait', *Umbrella*, published by Richard Demarco Gallery, vol. 1, no. 2, March 1972

Ali Smith, 'Margaret Tait', LUXONLINE tour, www.luxonline. org.uk, 2004

——, 'The Margaret Tait Years', in Peter Todd and Benjamin Cook (eds.) *Subjects and Sequences: A Margaret Tait Reader* (London: LUX, 2004), pp. 7–27

Felicity Sparrow, 'Garden Pieces', *Poem Film Film Poem*, no. 9, February 2001, pp. 1–2, doubled as programme notes for 'Garden Pieces', a film programme curated by Peter Todd

Robert Scott Speranza, 'The film-poem and its development: poetry and film from 1910–2003', PhD thesis, University of Sheffield 2003.

Gerda Stevenson, 'The Late Margaret Tait, Film-maker: An Appreciation', *The Orcadian*, 17 May 1999

——, 'Margaret Tait', obituary, *The Scotsman*, 5 May 1999

Elizabeth Sussex, 'Margaret Tait, Film-maker', *The Financial Times*, 9 September 1970

——, 'Margaret Tait', obituary, *The Guardian*, 13 May 1999, p. 22

Peter Todd, 'Bibliography on Margaret Tait', in *Experimental Film: 16+ Study Guide* (London: BFI, 2004), pp. 9–11

——, 'A Future Led by Looking', in Alistair Peebles and Laura Watts (eds.), *Orkney Futures* (Orkney: Brae Editions, 2009), p. 51

——, 'Margaret Tait', LUXONLINE essay, www.luxonline.org.uk, 2004

——, 'The Margaret Tait Project', *Media Education Journal*, 33, Spring 2003, pp. 27–30

——, 'Remote Lives?… Looking Beyond the Canon: The need for images that are local', *Vertigo*, vol. 2, no. 6, Spring 2004, p. 56

Peter Todd (ed.) 'Remembering Margaret Tait: A Deeper Knowledge Than Wisdom', *Vertigo*, vol. 2., no. 7, Autumn/Winter 2004, p. 53–5

Peter Todd and Benjamin Cook (eds.) *Subjects and Sequences: A Margaret Tait Reader* (London: LUX, 2004)

Joss Winn, 'Preserving the Handpainted Films of Margaret Tait', MA Dissertation, University of East Anglia, 2002, http://tait.josswinn.org

Angus Wolfe-Murray, '*Blue Black Permanent*', *The Scotsman Weekender*, 24 April 1993

Robert Yates, '*Blue Black Permanent*', review, *Sight and Sound*, April 1993, p. 43

Selected Filmography

The majority of Tait's films are held by the Scottish Screen Archive (see 'Archives', p. 178 below). LUX (www.lux.org.uk) also distributes her films and Freunde der Deutschen Kinemathek, Berlin (www.fdk-berlin.de) and the South London Poem Film Society (www.lux.org.uk) hold a few films for distribution.

The Lion, the Griffin, and the Kangaroo, 1951, with Peter Hollander, 13.33 mins, 16mm, black and white, sound

One is One, 1951, with Fernando Birri and Peter Hollander, 33.03 mins, 16mm, black and white, silent

Three Portrait Sketches, with Peter Hollander, 1951, 5.56 mins, 16mm, black and white, silent

A Portrait of Ga, 1952, 4.27 mins, 16mm, colour, sound

Happy Bees, 1954, 16.07 mins, 16mm, colour, sound

Calypso, 1955, 4.29 mins, 35mm, colour, sound

The Leaden Echo and the Golden Echo, 1955, 6.27 mins, 16mm, colour, sound

Orquil Burn, 1955, 35.40 mins, 16mm, colour, sound

Rose Street, 1956, assisted by Alex Pirie, 14.44 mins, 35mm, black and white, sound

Rose Street, 1956, 14.14 mins, 16mm, black and white, sound

The Drift Back, 1957, 10.56 mins, 16mm, black and white, sound

Hugh MacDiarmid, A Portrait, 1964, 8.27 mins, 16mm, black and white, sound

Palindrome, 1964, 3 mins, 16mm, black and white, sound

Where I Am Is Here, 1964, producer Alex Pirie, 32.48, 16 mm, black and white, sound

The Big Sheep (Caora Mor), 1966, 41.02 mins, 16 mm, black and white, sound

Splashing, 1966, 4.53 mins, 16mm, black and white, sound

A Pleasant Place, 1969, 21mins, 16mm, black and white, sound

He's Back (The Return), 1970, 20 mins, 16mm, sound

John Macfadyen (The Stripes in the Tartan), 1970, 3.30 mins, 16mm, colour, sound

Painted Eightsome, 1970, 6.16 mins, 35mm, colour, sound

Aerial, 1974, 4 mins, 16mm, black and white/colour, sound

Colour Poems, 1974, 11.20 mins, 16mm, colour, sound

On the Mountain, 1974, 32.33 mins, 16mm, black and white/colour, sound

These Walls, 1974, black and white/colour, silent

Place of Work, 1976, 31.11 mins, 16mm, colour, sound

Tailpiece, 1976, 9.23 mins, 16mm, black and white, sound

Aspects of Kirkwall: The Ba, 1965/75, 62.42 mins, 16mm, black and white/colour, sound

Aspects of Kirkwall: Occasions, 1977, 9.03 mins, 16mm, colour, sound

Aspects of Kirkwall: Shape of a Town, 1977, 7.49 mins, 16mm, colour, sound

Aspects of Kirkwall: The Look of the Place, 1981, 17 mins, 16mm, black and

white, sound
Aspects of Kirkwall: Some Changes, 1981, 21.38 mins, 16mm, colour, sound
Land Makar, 1981, 31.32 mins, 16mm, colour, sound
Blue Black Permanent, 1992, producer Barbara Grigor, Viz Productions, Channel 4, BFI, 84 mins, 35mm, colour, sound
Garden Pieces, 1998, 11.30 mins, 16mm, colour, sound

Two profiles focusing on Tait and her films were produced for television. Channel 4 also screened a selection of her films as part of the Eleventh Hour series in 1987.

Poet with a Camera, Spectrum, BBC Scotland, 30 mins, 5 January 1979, 10:15pm
Margaret Tait; Filmmaker, Channel 4 and the Arts Council of Great Britain, 35 mins, 25 April 1983
Eleventh Hour series, selection of films by Margaret Tait (including *Where I Am is Here*), Channel 4, 9 March 1987, 10.55pm

Archives

Scottish Screen Archive

39–41 Montrose Avenue
Hillington Park
Glasgow G52 4LA
www.nls.uk/ssa

The central archive for Tait's films. Viewing copies of most of her films are available, as are various paper archives relating to Tait and the Films of Scotland Committee. The Scottish Screen Archive website provides full details for her films, including archivists' viewing notes and allows visitors to view extracts from selected films.

Orkney Archive

The Orkney Library & Archive
44 Junction Road, Kirkwall
Orkney KW15 1AG
www.orkney.gov.uk

Forty-one boxes of material relating to Margaret Tait, including drafts of manuscripts, correspondence, photographs, notebooks, diaries, and production and promotional material. The archive also holds viewing copies of Tait's films, including her feature film, *Blue Black Permanent*. Recordings of Tait reading her poetry and a short film documenting the removal of material from her studio after her death are also available for

Poems, Stories and Writings

study purposes. A significant collection of Tait's notebooks will be added to the archive in 2012.

LUX

18 Shacklewell Lane
London E8 2EZ
www.luxonline.org.uk/artists/margaret_tait/index.html

The major distributor and resource for artist's films in the UK, LUX hold many of Tait's films in addition to two film programmes which are available for hire. They are also the publisher of Peter Todd and Benjamin Cook (eds.), *Subjects and Sequences: A Margaret Tait Reader* (2004) and the DVD *Margaret Tait: Selected Films: 1952–1976.* Their website provides a comprehensive introduction to the filmmaker, including bibliographies, filmographies, information on the films and essay contributions from the writer Ali Smith and the filmmaker Peter Todd.

Other relevant collections

BFI National Archive, London, www.bfi.org.uk/nationalarchive (copies of the two television profiles of Tait, *Poet with a Camera* and *Margaret Tait Filmmaker*)

BFI National Library, London, www.bfi.org.uk/filmtvinfo/library (published books and articles)

British Artists' Film and Video Study Collection at Central Saint Martins, University of the Arts, London, www.studycollection.org.uk (letters, paper documents and recorded talks)

National Library of Scotland, Edinburgh, www.nls.uk (letters from the MacDiarmid Collection)

The Pier Arts Centre, Stromness, Orkney, www.pierartscentre.com (a selection of Tait's films)

Scottish National Gallery of Modern Art, Edinburgh, www.natgalscot.ac.uk (letters from Richard Demarco archive)

The University of Stirling, www.film.stir.ac.uk/film-archives-collection (letters from the John Grierson and Lindsay Anderson archive)

Index of Poem Titles

Index of Poem First Lines

FyfieldBooks

Two millennia of essential classics

The extensive Fyfield*Books* list includes

Djuna Barnes *The Book of Repulsive Women and other poems*
edited by Rebecca Loncraine

Elizabeth Barrett Browning *Selected Poems* edited by Malcolm Hicks

Charles Baudelaire *Complete Poems in French and English*
translated by Walter Martin

The Brontë Sisters *Selected Poems*
edited by Stevie Davies

Lewis Carroll *Selected Poems*
edited by Keith Silver

Thomas Chatterton *Selected Poems*
edited by Grevel Lindop

John Clare *By Himself*
edited by Eric Robinson and David Powell

Samuel Taylor Coleridge *Selected Poetry* edited by William Empson and David Pirie

John Donne *Selected Letters*
edited by P.M. Oliver

Oliver Goldsmith *Selected Writings*
edited by John Lucas

Victor Hugo *Selected Poetry in French and English*
translated by Steven Monte

Wyndham Lewis *Collected Poems and Plays* edited by Alan Munton

Charles Lamb *Selected Writings*
edited by J.E. Morpurgo

Ben Jonson *Epigrams and The Forest*
edited by Richard Dutton

Giacomo Leopardi *The Canti with a selection of his prose*
translated by J.G. Nichols

Andrew Marvell *Selected Poems*
edited by Bill Hutchings

Charlotte Mew *Collected Poems and Selected Prose*
edited by Val Warner

Michelangelo *Sonnets*
translated by Elizabeth Jennings, introduction by Michael Ayrton

William Morris *Selected Poems*
edited by Peter Faulkner

Ovid *Amores*
translated by Tom Bishop

Edgar Allan Poe *Poems and Essays on Poetry*
edited by C.H. Sisson

Restoration Bawdy
edited by John Adlard

Rainer Maria Rilke *Sonnets to Orpheus and Letters to a Young Poet*
translated by Stephen Cohn

Christina Rossetti *Selected Poems*
edited by C.H. Sisson

Sir Walter Scott *Selected Poems*
edited by James Reed

Sir Philip Sidney *Selected Writings*
edited by Richard Dutton

Henry Howard, Earl of Surrey *Selected Poems*
edited by Dennis Keene

Algernon Charles Swinburne *Selected Poems*
edited by L.M. Findlay

Oscar Wilde *Selected Poems*
edited by Malcolm Hicks

Sir Thomas Wyatt *Selected Poems*
edited by Hardiman Scott

For more information, including a full list of Fyfield*Books* and a contents list for each title, and details of how to order the books, visit the Carcanet website at www.carcanet.co.uk or email info@carcanet.co.uk